USA TODAY bestselling and RITA® Award–winning author **Marie Ferrarella** has written more than two hundred and fifty books for Harlequin, some under the name Marie Nicole. Her romances are beloved by fans worldwide. Visit her website, marieferrarella.com.

Books by Marie Ferrarella

Harlequin Special Edition

Forever, Texas

The Cowboy's Lesson in Love

Matchmaking Mamas

Diamond in the Ruff
Her Red-Carpet Romance
Coming Home for Christmas
Dr. Forget-Me-Not
Twice a Hero, Always Her Man
Meant to Be Mine
A Second Chance for the Single Dad
Christmastime Courtship
Engagement for Two
Adding Up to Family

The Fortunes of Texas: The Secret Fortunes

Fortune's Second-Chance Cowboy

The Montana Mavericks: The Great Family Roundup

The Maverick's Return

The Fortunes of Texas: The Rulebreakers

The Fortune Most Likely To...

Visit the Author Profile page
at Harlequin.com for more titles.

Prologue

Connor Fortunado was torn.

He glanced out of the window of his first-class seat. The flight was just about over.

He was almost there.

Houston.

Home.

Connor half smiled to himself. Home, better known as "The House of the Incurable Romantics." The whimsical title had recently occurred to him because every one of his five siblings was either married or going to be married.

Except for him.

And that little fact of life, he promised himself, wasn't about to change anytime soon.

Or ever.

Connor was pretty happy with his life. He was thirty-one, single, carefree and able to take off at a moment's notice without an explanation to anyone if he wanted to—the way he had just done. If he were married and had what was whimsically referred to in some circles as "a better half," right about now that "better half" would most likely be giving him hell for the double life he was leading. She would have doubtlessly not looked favorably on his giving up an executive position with a prestigious corporate search firm just so that he could follow his passion.

Everyone in the family still thought he was that highly paid executive at his old firm. His former career had been a dependable, respectable position with an excellent, if somewhat boring, future laid out in front of it. None of his relatives knew that somewhere along the line he had discovered he had a real aptitude for detective work.

It had begun innocently enough. He'd helped his boss uncover an embezzling scheme within the company. But once he'd discovered the culprit, Connor found that he was hooked on the rush that came in the wake of untangling all the twisted skeins and getting to the bottom of the mystery. After a bit of soul-searching, he'd decided to put his newly honed skills to better use. So he had turned his back on the corporate world and became a highly paid private investigator.

Career changes like that wouldn't have sat well with a wife and she would have undoubtedly had no qualms about making her displeasure known.

To everyone.

Connor frowned. The moment of reckoning was almost here. He was going to have to come clean to his family once he landed in Houston. Telling his siblings should go fine because for the most part, they were pretty open-minded. It was coming clean to his parents that was going to be the problem. His parents, especially his father, were not going to look favorably on this change in careers.

He was *not* looking forward to this. All things considered, he would have gone on keeping his secret for as long as possible.

However, fate had other plans for him and was forcing him to own up to this major change in his life. All in the name of the family good. He just hoped his parents would see it that way. Yes, he was an adult, but there was still a part of him that preferred parental approval.

But he really didn't have the luxury of keeping this to himself any longer. His family needed him. There was no other conclusion to be reached.

Someone was out there, trying to get them.

It wasn't merely a paranoid thought reserved for the rich but an honest assessment of the situation. How else could he view what had been happening to different members of his family in the last two months? Like to his father's half brother. Gerald Robinson's estate, palatial by any standards, had been the target of an arsonist, set on fire and almost burned down to the ground. The family-based technology firm, Robinson Tech, had been the victim of cybersabotage. And Fortunado Real Estate, a company his father founded and two of his sisters and one of his brothers-in-law now worked at, had been the target of sabotage, as well.

It was as if no one who was even remotely related

to the Fortune family—no matter how they spelled their last name—was safe.

Connor had a gut feeling that it was only going to get worse unless whoever was responsible for wreaking all this havoc was found and captured. As a Fortunado, he had found that he and his family were related to the Fortunes. And that meant he couldn't just sit on the sidelines and watch this little drama play out.

He had to *do* something. He had natural skills, he had connections and he had the money to fund the investigation, all of which would serve him well in his search for whoever was attempting to carry out this vendetta against the entire Fortune family.

His family.

In his mind, Connor was already getting started on the case even though he was still airborne.

All he had to do, he thought, was get past telling his parents.

"Ladies and gentlemen, we will be beginning our descent to Houston shortly. Please return your tray tables to the upright positions…"

The cheerful flight attendant continued with her instructions, her voice fading into the background for Connor.

Connor's stomach felt just the slightest bit queasy. Not because of the airplane's descent, but because of what lay ahead.

Zero hour was almost here.

Chapter One

They walked into the big, sprawling living room en masse: his sister Valene; his sister Maddie and her husband, Zach McCarter; and his parents, Kenneth and Barbara Fortunado.

Here goes nothin', Connor thought, putting on his game face.

Kenneth Fortunado, a robust giant of a man, had never been known for beating around the bush. He got right to it.

"All right, Connor, what's the big mystery?" Kenneth asked his son as he came in. "What suddenly brings you here?"

"My guess is it has to be something big to get Connor to leave that cushy, high-paying executive job of his back in Denver and bring his butt back home,"

Maddie said, making herself comfortable on one of the oversize sofas in the room.

"It's not bad news, is it, dear?" Barbara Fortunado asked, her brown eyes wide with worry as they searched her son's face. "Please don't let it be bad news. I couldn't bear to hear about anything else bad happening after all that's been going on."

"Come to think of it, you do look rather unsettled, boy," Kenneth said, looking more closely at his son's face. "Out with it. What's going on? Why are you suddenly here?"

Unable to remain quiet any longer, Connor's sister Valene spoke up. "Everybody, let Connor breathe. We're all getting way too jumpy." Valene was referring to the fact that the place where they all worked, Fortunado Real Estate, had suddenly and inexplicably seen a turn for the worse in the last two months. They'd lost a good share of their best clients.

Taking Maddie's hand in his, Zach McCarter gave Connor a sympathetic look, as if to say that he was glad he wasn't the one in his brother-in-law's shoes, although for now he wisely remained silent.

Connor looked around the room. There were members of his immediate family who were missing from the gathering although he had put the word out that he wanted to speak to all of them at the same time. He saw no sense in having to go through this little drama twice, but obviously his message hadn't registered properly.

"I was hoping to say this when everyone was here," Connor told his father.

"You're going to have to settle for half the family,"

Kenneth told him, his tone already growing impatient. "In case you haven't noticed, trying to get everyone together in one place—apart from holding a wedding— is like herding cats—"

"More like herding chickens," Valene said under her breath, then flashed a smile at her father when Kenneth shot her a look. It was obvious she hadn't thought she was going to be overheard.

"Connor, please tell us," Barbara entreated her son. "You're getting me very nervous."

Feeling guilty that he was adding to his mother's concerns, Connor stopped stalling. Half a family was better than none.

Taking a deep breath, he launched into the reason for his unexpected return home.

Connor started slowly. "It's nothing to make you nervous, Mother."

"Spit it out, Connor," Kenneth ordered. "If you beat around the bush like this at that corporate search firm of yours, it's a wonder that they haven't shown you the door yet."

This was as good an opening as any, Connor thought. "Well, that's part of what I wanted to talk to you about," he began.

Kenneth cut him off. "They fired you?" he cried, astonished despite what he'd just said.

"No," Connor replied firmly. "They didn't fire me, but I'm not working for them anymore."

His father's complexion was turning a shade of unflattering red. "What do you mean you're not working for them anymore?" Kenneth demanded.

"Kenneth, please, let him speak," Barbara pleaded,

putting her hand on her husband's arm as if she was trying to gentle a wild stallion. "I'm sure he has a good explanation for all this." She looked at her son hopefully. Waiting.

"Well?" Kenneth demanded, his eyes all but pinning Connor against the wall.

Connor took in another breath, as if that would somehow shield him from the explosion he sensed was coming. "I'm not with that firm anymore because I'm a private investigator now."

"You're a PI?" Maddie cried in awed disbelief. Suddenly, a smile bloomed on her lips. "You mean like Magnum?"

Valene looked at her sister, lost. "Who's Magnum?" she wanted to know.

"Some guy on a classic TV show," Zach volunteered. "I caught a few episodes on one of those channels that show nothing but programs from the seventies and eighties."

"No, not like Magnum," Connor corrected tolerantly. "Most of the work isn't as glamorous as TV makes it out to be. It requires a lot of patience and a great deal of attention to detail," he told his family, hoping that was enough.

Apparently, it wasn't. Exasperated, Kenneth waved his hand for everyone else in the room to be quiet. He obviously intended to go toe to toe with his son.

"You're a *private eye*?" Kenneth cried, completely stunned and grossly disappointed. There was no question of that. "What the hell were you thinking?"

"It's 'private investigator,' Dad," Connor told his father patiently. "And what I was thinking was that maybe I could help find out who's responsible for everything that's been going on around here lately."

"There are professionals for that sort of thing, dear," Barbara told her son, speaking up.

Connor turned to look at his mother. He hadn't thought this was going to be easy, he reminded himself. "I *am* a professional, Mother."

Kenneth let out an exasperated breath. "Since when?" he mocked.

Connor turned his attention to his father. He couldn't back down now. If he did, it was all over. "Since a few months ago."

Kenneth frowned, shaking his head, unable to accept the information or come to grips with it.

"I don't believe you," Kenneth countered. "You wouldn't do something that was so life-altering without telling me."

"I *am* telling you," Connor pointed out. "Now. There was no reason to say anything earlier."

It was plain to everyone that Kenneth found the explanation entirely unacceptable.

"How did this happen?" his father wanted to know. "Did you wake up one morning and just say, 'Gee, I'm tired of my high-paying executive job. Let me throw it all away and do something totally mindless, like become a private eye.' Is that what happened?" Kenneth demanded hotly.

"Private detective, dear," Barbara corrected her husband.

"Private *investigator*," Connor said calmly, correcting them both. "And no, I didn't just wake up one morning and decide to become a private investigator," he told

his father. "My boss suspected that there was someone embezzling money from the firm, but he didn't
know how to go about finding out who was behind it.
He shared his concern with me and I told him I'd do a
little snooping around. I did and as it turns out, I discovered who was stealing the firm's money in a little
less than a week."

Kenneth dourly dismissed the accounting. "You
got lucky."

"No, I didn't," Connor informed his father. "I was
persistent. And I found that I had a natural aptitude
for ferreting things out."

Kenneth snorted. "My son the Ferret. I can't wait
to tell people your new job description."

"Dad, you're missing the point here," Valene insisted,
looking at her father with a touch of annoyance as she
came to her brother's aid. "Connor said he was here to
help us get to the bottom of what's been happening to
the family lately."

She looked at her father, waiting for her words to
sink in.

"That's for the police to do," Barbara reminded her
children. No doubt she didn't like the idea of any of her
children getting involved with something that could
be dangerous.

"And how far have they gotten with their investigation?" Maddie challenged her mother.

Barbara raised her shoulders in a helpless shrug,
then offered an excuse to Maddie. "It's still early,"
Barbara said.

"Do you really want to wait until someone's killed

before we do anything, Mother?" Connor asked his mother gently.

Barbara's eyes widened, as if she hadn't thought about that possibility. "Do you really think that could happen?" she asked Connor.

His inclination was to shelter his mother, but he had to be honest. "The way things are escalating, there's no reason to believe that it couldn't."

Kenneth was still unconvinced. "Okay, hotshot, let's hear it. What's your big 'theory' about what's been going on?" the senior Fortunado asked. "Do you even have one?"

Mindful that his father was judging every word out of his mouth, Connor began slowly, speaking distinctly. "I think that these aren't just random acts the way the police initially thought." He paused for a half beat, looking at each of them before delivering his bombshell. "I think there's one person behind everything that's been happening."

Kenneth's eyes squinted as he regarded his son. "You're talking about the fire, the hacking and the sabotaging of the real estate dealings?" he wanted to know.

"Yes," Connor replied stoically.

"One person is behind all this?" Zach asked, wanting to get his facts clear.

Relieved to hear a nonjudgmental voice, Connor glanced at Maddie's husband. "Yes, that's what I'm thinking."

"That must be one very energetic person," Kenneth commented. The sarcasm was hard to miss.

"People can be hired to carry out these things. But I

believe there's one person orchestrating all these things being executed against the family," Connor told them.

As he looked around at their faces, Connor could see that his mother and sisters, as well as Zach, were more than willing to be convinced. His father, however, was still digging in his heels. Whether it was because the man didn't agree with the theory or because he was angry over the fact that Connor had suddenly switched careers, Connor didn't know.

He waited for his father to say something. He didn't have long to wait.

"And just who is this vengeful person targeting the family?" Kenneth wanted to know. "Do you know, or is this all just one big theory you're hoping to get us to buy into?"

Connor kept his eyes on his father as he answered. "I found evidence of rumormongering."

"You're going to have to explain that to me," his mother said. "What does rumormongering mean?"

Kenneth began to open his mouth, undoubtedly to define the term for his wife, but Connor was already explaining it to his mother in what he felt would be simpler terms than his father was wont to use.

"Someone has been bad-mouthing Fortunado Real Estate's dealings on the internet, Mother, causing business to drop. Because of the so-called rumors, people have withdrawn their business from the company and taken it elsewhere."

"And does this 'someone' have a name?" Kenneth asked again, his impatient tone suggesting that he sincerely doubted his son had gotten that far in his so-called "investigation."

Connor managed to surprise his father, as well as his mother, by answering, "Yes."

"Well?" Kenneth asked, waiting to hear who this person was.

"From everything I've managed to learn, I believe the person who's causing all this chaos is Charlotte Prendergast Robinson."

"Gerald's wife?" Barbara cried, astonished at the revelation.

"Uncle Gerald's *ex*-wife," Connor corrected his mother. It was being Gerald's ex that had caused the woman to launch her vendetta in the first place, he believed.

Kenneth looked at his son skeptically, although in all truthfulness, the woman's name had been mentioned in connection to all these acts once or twice before.

"I know that Charlotte's angry," his father began, rolling the idea over in his mind.

"She's way more than that, Dad," Valene interjected. "You know that line about a woman scorned," she reminded her father.

"Val's right," Maddie said, adding her voice to her sister's as well as Connor's. "Aunt Charlotte wasn't exactly a hundred percent stable before Uncle Gerald finally left her to go back with that woman he called his first love, Deborah. Think about it," Maddie stressed. "I mean, who in their right mind puts together a whole big binder devoted to her husband's illegitimate children?" She shook her head at the very thought.

"Maybe the woman just wanted to have a book devoted to her family's genealogy," Barbara said. Connor knew his mother was always ready to see the good in everyone.

"More like having a book she could use to blackmail everyone," Maddie said. "Besides, I doubt she thinks of the people in that binder as 'her' family. It's more like his family—not that Uncle Gerald even knew some of them existed until Charlotte got started collecting names."

"I wouldn't put anything past Aunt Charlotte," Connor told the others.

"I think it was finding out that Deborah was the mother of his triplets that did it," Maddie suggested. "It was the last straw, the thing that finally unhinged Charlotte."

"Why would that do it any more than knowing about the other illegitimate ones?" Kenneth asked. He frowned. It was obvious that he didn't like or welcome the fact that he was actually related to Gerald. "That man spread his seed more than anyone ever cited in the Bible," he said with disgust.

"Kenneth," Barbara chided, obviously surprised at her husband saying something like that.

"Well, it's true," Kenneth told his wife. "He didn't care who he impregnated. The man should have been neutered."

"Are you *sure* we're actually related to Gerald Robinson?" Maddie asked. "Maybe there was some mistake made."

Connor sympathized with his sister's desire to sever ties, but it wasn't that simple. "Dad and Gerald are both Grandpa Julius's sons," he pointed out.

"We're half brothers," Kenneth corrected tersely. "For what that's worth."

"That was when Gerald was still known as Jerome Fortune, before he decided to run off and assume another complete identity," Barbara explained to her children, no doubt to keep things straight in case the fact had gotten lost among the preponderance of offspring who had been discovered.

Maddie squinted as if she was trying to reconcile a few facts with ones that already existed. "Wait, my head hurts," she said as she dramatically put her hand to her forehead.

Valene laughed at her sister's theatrics as she shook her own head. "One thing I have to say about this family. We are definitely not boring."

"No, Gerald and his extended family aren't boring," Kenneth corrected with feeling. "We are just an average, run-of-the-mill family with some decent monetary holdings," he insisted. "Or we were," he said as he looked in Connor's direction, "until one of my sons decided to completely turn his life inside out and become a—" his eyes met Connor's "—PI," Kenneth concluded.

Connor wanted to put this behind them once and for all. His father had to understand that his new career would only help the family in the long run, not embarrass it. "Dad, you're getting off track here," Connor respectfully pointed out.

"And your 'track' is that this was all done by Charlotte as her way of getting even, is that it?" Kenneth asked.

"Yes," Connor answered simply.

"But why would she do all this?" Kenneth asked. "Wouldn't her vengeance be focused directly on Gerald, not the rest of the family?" He rethought his words. "Or better yet, on Deborah? After all, in Charlotte's warped mind wouldn't she think Deborah is responsible for stealing her husband away from her?" Kenneth insisted.

There was no simple, hard-and-fast answer to that. "I think we can all agree that Aunt Charlotte is a complicated person. I wouldn't begin to try to analyze exactly what's on her mind. I would be lost in that maze for days," Connor predicted.

"And yet you think she's the one behind this?" Barbara asked her son.

The two were not mutually exclusive. "Yes, I do," Connor answered.

"She might be a cold, vengeful person, but she is still family, Connor. I really don't think she'd go to such great lengths to get back at Gerald or Jerome or whatever he wants to call himself," Barbara argued.

"Well, Mother, I'm not as kindhearted as you. And according to the evidence I've found, she is definitely mixed up in this, if not the actual orchestrator—which I actually believe she is."

Connor looked around at his family in silence, allowing his words to sink in. Hoping he had finally gotten them to see the situation the way he did.

He was convinced the only hope they had was to fight this as a united front.

Chapter Two

"One question." Kenneth moved to the edge of the sofa he was sitting on, raising his hand as if he was a student in a classroom instead of the former CEO of Fortunado Real Estate.

"Only one?" Connor asked, unable to keep the amused expression off his face.

"One's enough," Kenneth responded sternly. "Charlotte Robinson seems to have done a disappearing act—"

"I know that," Connor answered, anticipating his father's question. "Which is why I'm planning on finding her."

Kenneth waved a hand at his son's declaration, for all intents and purposes dismissing it.

"And therein lies my question," Kenneth replied. "There are countless people trying to track this woman down, from the local police to the FBI to even our illustrious matriarch herself, Kate Fortune, who you might remember, despite being in her nineties, is one exceptionally formidable woman. With the boundless resources that are at Kate's disposal, if she can't find Charlotte, what in hell makes you think that you're going to be able to do anything different?" his father wanted to know.

"I'm not an egotist, Dad," Connor replied mildly. "I don't think that I'm the only one who can find Charlotte. It's just that," he continued despite the cynical look on his father's face, "sometimes I wind up getting results by thinking outside the box. Besides, the more people putting their heads together and working on locating Charlotte Robinson, the greater the chances are of actually bringing her to justice."

Kenneth blew out a breath. "I suppose I can't argue with that."

"Give him time," Valene said to Connor with a wink. "He'll find a way."

She went on in a louder voice, clapping her hands together to get everyone's attention. "Okay, now that we've all been told about Connor's new career and all agreed that Connor should try to find that awful woman before she does anything else, possibly even more reprehensible, to the family, let's get back to our favorite topic."

Connor looked at his sister quizzically. "And that would be—?"

"An engagement party," she answered him gleefully, her eyes dancing as a broad smile slipped over her lips, curving them.

Connor closed his eyes. Engagements and weddings. His least favorite topics of conversation in the world. "I think that's my cue to exit, stage right."

But before he could take a single step to make that happen, Maddie linked her arm through his.

"Not today, brother dear. Mother told me that you're spending the night at the old homestead," she said, gesturing around the area, which couldn't by any stretch of the imagination be referred to as "the old homestead," at least not if accuracy was a factor.

"Looks to me like you're trapped," Zach told his brother-in-law, traces of amused compassion in his voice.

"Trapped? No, no offense, Zach, but that's one thing I'm never going to be." Connor shook his head as he glanced at his sisters and thought about his missing siblings, all of whom were undoubtedly with their "significant other" at the moment. "You know, I really can't get over how domesticated everyone's gotten over this past year and a half."

"Yeah, yeah, your time'll come," Valene predicted, letting Connor know that she wasn't buying into this act of his.

However, Connor remained steadfast because he honestly believed that his status was never going to change. "Sorry, not going to happen. Not to me."

"Just because you're the last man standing, brother dear, doesn't mean you're going to stay that way," Maddie told him.

"You're right," Connor answered his sister. "I *am* the last man standing. And I intend to keep on standing for a very long, long time."

"What do you have against being happy?" Zach asked Connor as he slipped his arm around Maddie's shoulders and drew her closer to him.

"But that's just my point," Connor told the other man. "I *am* happy. I *like* being free and not accountable to anyone except for myself. And you people on occasion," he added as an afterthought, looking around at the others in the living room.

Barbara Fortunado merely smiled at her son as she reached over and patted his cheek affectionately. "Your time will come, dear," was all she said before she turned her attention to her daughters.

A moment later, she became fully immersed in finalizing plans for the wedding—which at this point was only a month away.

Connor turned to look at his father, who from what he could determine was also standing on the outskirts of this conversation, the way he was.

Yes, he thought, romance was all well and good, but when that faded and the day-to-day business of living had to be addressed, that was where it all fell apart. He liked keeping things fresh, not facing the same old stale fare day in, day out. In his opinion, marriages were about routines and he liked to mix things up.

"You understand, right, Dad?" Connor asked the man sitting across from him.

"Do I understand how you feel right at this moment? Yes, I do," Kenneth admitted freely.

Connor was glad to hear that he had his father's support. "Well, at least you can see that—"

"I also understand," Kenneth went on as if his son

hadn't said anything, "that all that'll change the moment the right woman comes into your life."

"Lots of women have come into my life, Dad," Connor pointed out. That was part of the joy of being unattached. "And I'm still free."

"I said the *right* woman," Kenneth emphasized. "And it's not something anyone can convince you of until it actually happens to you," his father said knowingly. "Until then," he counseled, "just enjoy thinking that you're happy."

Connor merely offered his father a smile. He knew he couldn't change his father's mind any more than his father could change his. But he *was* happy, Connor thought with conviction. He knew that. And he intended to remain that way no matter what anyone else might think to the contrary.

But because the upcoming wedding seemed to make his sister so happy, he remained in the room and pretended to listen to all the plans that were being made for the anticipated nuptials.

He even nodded and smiled in the right places while his thoughts were elsewhere.

"Do you need anything, Connor?" Barbara Fortunado asked her son much later that evening.

Talks regarding the wedding plans had gone on much longer than anyone had thought they would and time had just gotten away from them. To his credit, she thought, Connor had feigned interest and even contributed a word or two, which made his sisters happy. It was nice seeing her children getting along.

She paused now to look in on her son, who was spending the night in what had once been his bedroom.

"No, I'm good, Mom," Connor told her. Sitting on the edge of the bed, he looked around the room. It had been a long time since he'd been here. "Although I have to admit that it feels a little strange to be back here after all this time," he confessed.

Barbara nodded. Like all good mothers, she realized that her children had to make their own way in the world and she was proud of each and every one of them. But there were times when their very success at forging their paths out in the world made her feel just a little sad. There were times, fleeting moments actually, when she longed for the days that they had all been together, under one roof, and needed her.

She smiled at Connor now. "It's nice to have you back, even if it is for just a little while and even if the reason you're here is because this nasty business was what drew you back." Her mouth quirked a little. "No matter what the reason, you're here and that's all I care about."

Connor crossed the room to the doorway where his mother was standing. Slipping his arm around her shoulders, he pressed a kiss to her temple.

"You were—and are—the primary draw that brought me back, Mom. You always have been."

Barbara laughed softly. "You always did have a way with words. Not always a truthful way, I grant you, but always sweet," she concluded. And then she became his mother again as he crossed back to his bed. "Get some sleep, dear."

Connor couldn't help grinning at her. "I am thirty-one, you know."

Barbara nodded, as if she had heard all this before and was prepared for it. "And you'll always be my little boy no matter what age you are. Good night, Connor."

Connor inclined his head obligingly. "Good night, Mom," he replied.

He waited until his mother had closed his bedroom door behind her. Getting up off the bed, he crossed over to his desk and took out the folder he had slipped into the top drawer. Pulling out his chair, he sat down at the desk and began to go through the folder. It was filled with notes he'd made to himself regarding Charlotte Robinson's dealings, as well as her possible current whereabouts.

He reviewed his notes slowly, rereading everything as if it was the first time he was seeing it. In his compilations, he'd come across the name of a freelance researcher, a Brianna Childress, who had handled some work for Charlotte Robinson over the course of the previous year.

He looked at the papers thoughtfully. Whatever this Brianna person had been doing for Charlotte had to have been sent to some address, even if that address turned out to be a PO box. That PO box in turn had to have been paid for, which meant that there'd been a check that could be traced to a bank account.

In addition, this freelancer had to be paid for her trouble. That brought him back to the bank account again, or at least a traceable credit card. All this meant that there was a possible paper trail. One he intended to follow.

It was a start, Connor told himself.

"You don't know it yet, Brianna Childress, but you are about to be paid a visit tomorrow morning," he said aloud. He closed the folder but went on holding it in his hands a little longer, as if the act connected him to the woman he was pursuing. "You just might be instrumental in helping me find the elusive Charlotte Prendergast Robinson before she can do any more damage."

Connor doubted that it would be that easy, but at least it was a lead, and who knew—maybe he'd get lucky. At the very least, this Childress woman might be able to provide him with the name of someone else who could in turn give him some clue as to where Charlotte Robinson was currently hiding.

He'd had less to go on before, he thought as he rose from the desk and got ready for bed.

Connor was up early the following morning and got dressed quickly.

He looked at the address he'd left out on his desk. It was the address where he was going to find this Childress woman. Initially, for about a minute and a half, he considered calling her to tell her he was coming to see her today.

He decided against it.

A face-to-face meeting would be the better way to go. He needed all the help he could get and the element of surprise might very well be useful in this case. If this woman turned out to be as nefarious as Charlotte, calling her might cause her to flee. If this Childress woman was actually involved with Charlotte, the last thing he wanted to do was tip her off.

He knew nothing about Brianna Childress, which meant that there was no reason to suppose that she *wouldn't* warn Charlotte that he was looking for her. That in turn would send Charlotte into even deeper hiding.

He wouldn't put anything past Charlotte no matter how innocent his parents, especially his mother, thought she was.

Since it was rather early, Connor decided to just slip out of the house without waking anyone.

The sooner he was on the road, the closer he would be to possibly bringing all this to a satisfactory conclusion.

He had another reason to get out of the house without being noticed. He didn't want to get involved in a possible discussion with his mother about Charlotte Robinson. Barbara Fortunado seemed reluctant to think badly of the other woman, but then, his mother had a tendency to view everyone in a good light.

However, there was no doubt in his mind that Charlotte was behind everything that had gone wrong in his family lately. She was a dangerous woman. The very fact that she had either tried to burn down Gerald Robinson's estate or had hired an arsonist to do it for her said it all in his book.

The woman was evil and the sooner he found her, the sooner he would rest easy.

Connor made good his escape and got to his car without anyone seeing him. Loading the address he'd found for Brianna Childress—the location was unfamiliar to him—into his car's GPS, he got started.

He turned on his radio but hardly heard any of

the music coming out of it. He was completely focused on the encounter that was ahead of him.

Connor expected the address of the research company he was looking for to lead him to an office building somewhere in Houston. Instead, the address wound up leading him to what appeared to be a rather small, homey-looking cottage.

Puzzled, he stopped his car a few hundred feet away from the house, wondering if he had made some sort of a mistake copying the address down.

Still, he thought, he was here so he might as well check it out.

Who knew, maybe this Brianna Childress ran her business out of her house. She wouldn't have been the first person to start out that way. The names of several computer companies and software firms came to mind.

Making up his mind, Connor started his car again. He brought it up closer to the cottage, then stopped a second time and parked.

Getting out, he made his way up the front walk. He noticed that there were some sort of bushes planted in the front yard. He wasn't very good at recognizing plants, although to his credit he did know a rose from a lily, he thought with a disparaging smile.

He saw neither in the yard.

Walking up to the front door, he noted that it was in need of a fresh coat of paint. Shrugging, he rang the doorbell. In his mind, he rehearsed what he planned to say to Brianna Childress in order to get her to let him come inside her house.

His finger had no sooner pressed the doorbell than the front door flew open.

A rather frazzled young woman with reddish-brown hair and heart-melting brown eyes looked up at him as if he was her personal savior. She was wearing jeans and a T-shirt, both of which lovingly highlighted all of her curves and nearly made him permanently lose his train of thought.

He recognized the woman from her online photo. But to be honest, she could use a new head shot. That one didn't do her justice.

"Oh thank goodness you're here!" Brianna cried, a look of relief washing over her features. "It's right in there!"

She pointed toward the back of the house where "it," whatever that referred to, was.

Without waiting for a response from him, Brianna grabbed his hand and pulled him in her wake, quickly leading him toward the back of the house.

Given that she had rather a good grip for such a delicate person, Connor realized that at the moment, he had no choice but to follow her.

"I was at my wits' end," Brianna confided unabashedly. "Luckily, I saw your ad on TV the other day and remembered the phone number. Actually, I copied it down," she confessed. "I had a feeling I was going to need you sooner rather than later and I was right. If you hadn't come, I'd probably be underwater before noon."

"Um—"

At a loss, Connor got no further. He had followed the woman into a bathroom. The "it" she was obviously referring to was a toilet. The water was rising precariously high within the bowl. It looked as if any second, the water was going to overflow and go all over the floor.

The sprightly redhead was standing in front of the toilet, her hands on her hips. "Kids," she said to him by way of an explanation.

"Kids?" Connor echoed, unable to understand what she was telling him.

"Every time I turn around, one of them has decided that one of their stuffed animals or trucks or figurines is dirty and needs to be washed. I guess the toilet's like a bathtub to them." She sighed and looked at him plaintively. "So, can you fix it?" she asked, a hopeful look on her face.

It was a face, Connor realized, that he couldn't bring himself to say no to.

Chapter Three

Connor forced himself to focus on something other than Brianna Childress's very expressive eyes. He knew that he couldn't very well lie to the woman, not if he needed her help and wanted her to be truthful with him. If he lied, or omitted telling her the truth, that wouldn't exactly be starting off their relationship, however short it might turn out to be, on the right foot. Lies just begat lies.

"I'm afraid that you've made a mistake," Connor began.

Dismay washed over Brianna's face as she took in what he had just said. "You can't fix it like the commercial said?" she asked.

"It's not that, it's—"

Connor got no further in his explanation than those first four words because right at that moment there was a bloodcurdling scream followed by a wail and then the sound of things either falling or being thrown.

The jarring noise went clear down to the bone.

"Oh dear lord, now what?" Brianna cried in exasperation.

Before Connor could venture a guess, she made an abrupt about-face and dashed out of the room, heading toward the scream. That left Connor standing alone in the bathroom with a toilet that looked as if it was about to blow at any moment.

"There's obviously never a dull moment around here," he commented under his breath.

Left to his own devices, Connor looked around the small, blue-and-white-tiled bathroom. From what he had gathered, this wasn't the first time the toilet presented a problem. Judging from the tools that were scattered on the floor, Brianna had the right things to deal with the situation.

The fact that she hadn't dealt with it told him that she'd never learned how to put any of these tools to use. She'd probably just seen the plumber using them and had thought ahead—or wanted to be prepared for the next time. Next time had obviously arrived.

He gave the woman an A for observation. Too bad her execution was sorely lacking.

Connor had no desire to follow the woman into the other room, given the high-pitched screaming that was coming from another part of the house, but on the other hand, he was never much for standing around gathering dust, either.

Looking around again, he took inventory of the tools in the room. There was a long, thin metallic tool expressly made for breaking through the debris that gathered in clogged pipes. Whimsically dubbed a "snake," it was lying beside a standard plunger. There were a couple of other tools, as well, but in his opinion, they were just overkill.

Connor prided himself on being rather handy. He decided that he might as well do *something* while he waited for the woman to come back.

Assessing the problem one last time, he rolled up his sleeves and got to work.

The job turned out to be easier than he had expected. The reason for the clog was a miniature toy train that had been wedged in the bottom of the toilet's evacuation pipe. The train had been covered in what appeared to be a massive wad of sopping wet toilet paper that had wound itself around the toy. It had been a little tricky getting the train free, but in the end, he managed to get it loose—all without breaking the toy.

He looked down at the item that was now safely nestled in his hand. *Such a little thing, so much trouble*, he thought.

It was only when he finally rose back to his feet again that he realized the knees of his pants had gotten quite wet. He looked around for a mop to at least dry the floor, but it appeared to be the one thing that the woman hadn't brought out with the other equipment.

Shaking his head, Connor muttered under his breath. "It figures."

"What figures?"

The voice startled him. Swinging around to face the doorway, he saw that Brianna had finally reappeared.

She was not alone. She was carrying a squirming, very vocal preschooler on her hip. A boy.

The slightly surprised look on her face gave way to a wide, relieved smile when she saw the toy train in Connor's hand.

"You fixed it," she cried, delighted.

The little boy on her hip saw the toy at the same time that his mother did.

"Mine!" he cried, eagerly putting his hands out as if that would somehow cause the toy to levitate out of the stranger's hand and into his own.

"Then what's it doing in the toilet?" Connor asked, pretending to be serious as he presented the train to the little boy after rinsing it off in the sink.

The kid had the same wide, sunny smile that his mother had. He flashed that smile now at Connor as he grabbed the toy train and pressed it to his chest.

"Mine," he repeated.

"We've established that," Connor replied as if he was talking to someone his own age. "But why did you—?"

Brianna anticipated his question. "You're not going to get an answer," she told him. "He knows he's not supposed to throw anything down there but for some reason, the toilet just seems to really fascinate him." She looked at her son with an indulgent smile. "Axel used to have a pet hamster until one day he decided that Howard was dirty and needed a bath."

"Let me guess," Connor said to her, "Howard drowned."

She surprised him by saying, "No, actually, he

didn't. I managed to fish him out of the toilet bowl just in time."

"So you saved Howard," Connor concluded.

"No," she said with a heartfelt sigh. "I didn't." When he raised a quizzical brow, she told him the rest of the story. "As near as I can figure it, Howard died of a heart attack. After I rescued him and dried him off, I put Howard in his cage. I found him the next morning, lying on the floor of the cage, as stiff as one of the kids' figurines."

The boy had stopped making noise and now sniffled a couple of times.

"We had a funeral," Axel said solemnly.

"So he *can* talk in sentences," Connor marveled, looking at the boy. The boy seemed pretty young to him and he had no idea just what kids were able to do at any given age.

"Only when he wants to," Brianna answered. Shifting her son to her other hip, she looked contritely at the man whose pant legs she had just noticed were wet. "I'm sorry I'm going on and on here. I don't get much of a chance to talk to adults," she admitted. Setting Axel down, she looked around for her purse. "How much do I owe you?"

Smiling at the woman, Connor shook his head. "Nothing."

Brianna looked at him, confused. "But you just fixed my toilet—and got your knees wet in the process," she pointed out.

"That's okay," he told her, shrugging off her offer of payment. "This is on me. No charge."

That only managed to confuse things even further

for Brianna. "I don't think your boss is going to appreciate you doing things for free."

"On the contrary," Connor said. He thought of his father, who he was, in essence, working for at the moment while he was conducting this investigation. "I think he'd approve."

Judging by her expression, his answer made absolutely no sense to the woman. "But you're a plumber. How are you supposed to make any money if you don't accept payment for doing a job?" she asked, confused.

"Because," Connor answered cavalierly, "I'm not a plumber."

This was making less and less sense to her. She began at the beginning. "But the company I called, they said they were sending someone right out."

"They probably meant what they said, but they didn't send me," he told her.

Things were finally falling into place. Brianna looked at the man standing and dripping in her bathroom. She was horrified at her mistake. He probably thought she was an idiot.

"I'm so embarrassed," she confessed, "I don't even know where to begin."

Amused, Connor laughed off her attempt at an apology. "Don't worry about it," he told her. "It was just an honest mistake."

The fact that she had let a perfect stranger into her house and that he was still standing here suddenly registered with her.

"But if you're not the plumber," she cried, backing away from him, "who are you?"

She was doing her best not to panic or appear nervous. After all, she had no idea who this man was or what he was doing in her house.

Brianna thought of her children and a chill went shooting up her spine.

She had to protect them!

Connor offered her an easy smile as he put his hand out to her. "Connor Fortunado, at your service."

But who was Connor Fortunado and why had he come to her house? His answer just created more questions.

Before she could ask him, the doorbell rang. For a split second, she appeared torn between questioning the man in her bathroom further or going to answer the doorbell.

The doorbell won.

Making up her mind, she hurried to the front of the house.

"Does it ever let up?" Connor called after her, curious.

"Sometimes," she answered. *Just not today.*

Brianna opened the door and found herself looking at a slightly overweight man in coveralls that had seen better days.

"Somebody called for a plumber?" he asked her.

"Yes, I did, but I don't need you anymore," Brianna began, ready to close the door again.

The man looked at her skeptically, then glanced down at what was apparently a work order in his hand. "The toilet fixed itself?" he asked with a touch of sarcasm.

"No, but—"

Connor was about to intervene for her but Brianna's

son beat him to it. Or, more accurately, her son and her daughter did. The duo had decided to resume whatever battle they had been deeply embroiled in a few minutes earlier.

Connor came forward, listening. The battle was apparently over whether or not the rather scrappy-looking mutt who had come running in with them should be wearing a dress. The vote was tied. The little girl—Ava, according to the name her brother had yelled—was saying yes while Axel was very loudly proclaiming, "No! He's a boy dog!"

Their supposedly small voices were completely drowning out the plumber, who, judging by the disgruntled look on his face, was protesting being sent away without collecting a fee. The fact that he hadn't done any work didn't seem to matter.

Meanwhile Connor found himself fascinated by the dynamics of the household he had walked into. Besides the scrappy dog, by his count he had glimpsed two cats and some sort of creature—a sea turtle perhaps?—living in a tank in the far corner of the living room. All he could really make out were a pair of eyes looking in his direction.

Connor's attention was drawn back to the squabbling children, who were growing progressively louder with each passing minute. Glancing in their mother's direction, he thought that she definitely looked overwhelmed. Taking pity on the woman, Connor decided to distract the children so that she could at least clear things up with the plumber.

"Gimme that!" Axel shouted, grabbing a frayed dress from his sister.

Though small, Ava was every bit as strong as her brother.

"No!" she cried, pulling the dress back out of her brother's hands.

Connor thought of physically pulling them apart but decided that he'd get more accomplished if he treated them as short adults, not discipline problems.

"You know," he began, "my brothers and sisters and I once dressed up our horse for Halloween." He had to raise his voice above theirs in order to actually be heard.

Axel stopped trying to pull the dress away from his sister. Meanwhile Ava's eyes widened as she suddenly became aware that there was someone besides her brother in the room.

"You dressed up your horse?" the little girl questioned, looking up at the strange man in her living room. Though she appeared a year or so younger than her brother, she was more articulate than Axel was.

"We sure did," Connor told her, subtly coaxing the brother and sister away from the front of the house and the plumber. The dog decided to trot along with them, as well. "My sisters wanted to put a ballerina costume on Lightning but my brothers and I said that the ballerina costume would just embarrass him."

"Who won?" Axel wanted to know. He gave his sister a superior look. "Bet it was the boys."

"Bet it wasn't," Ava countered, ready to get into yet another argument with him. "Everybody knows that boys are dumb."

"No they're not!" Axel yelled back.

"Actually," Connor said, raising his voice as he took

each of them by the hand and brought them toward the kitchen, "Lightning won."

"The horse?" Axel questioned, scrunching up his forehead.

"How could the horse win?" Ava wanted to know. "Could he talk?" she asked in awe.

"No, he wasn't a talking horse," Connor managed to say with a straight face.

"Then how did he win?" Axel asked, crossing his arms before his small chest and waiting to be given an answer.

"Lightning won because he got to keep his dignity," Connor told his small audience.

Ava and Axel exchanged perplexed looks. "What's dig-nitee?" Axel asked.

"Being proud of yourself," Connor explained.

Intrigued, Ava asked, "How did the horse get to keep that?"

"Well, Lightning was a boy horse," Connor told them. "We put a pirate's costume on him, using some of my mother's scarves. We all agreed that he looked a lot better in that than he would have in a ballerina costume. Besides," Connor confided, lowering his voice and winking at the children, "the tutu would have really been impossible to get on Lightning."

The abbreviated reference to the ballerina costume seemed to tickle Axel and he started to laugh. He laughed so hard, he wound up rolling around on the floor. The sound was infectious and it set Ava off. In no time flat, both children were on the floor, holding their sides and laughing.

Which was how Brianna found them when she walked into the kitchen.

The sight astounded her. For once, her children were actually getting along and no longer at each other's throats. Brianna stood for a moment, drinking in the sight.

Stunned, she looked at the man who was apparently responsible for her kids' miraculous about-face. She was both amazed that this Connor Fortunado had somehow managed to calm her little hellions down and horrified that she had allowed a total stranger to come into her house.

Allowed? She'd literally dragged him in, Brianna thought, berating herself.

Okay, there'd been a mix-up, which caused her to make the mistake, but even so, she'd let a stranger into her house. The house where her children lived. The man could have been an ax murderer or a serial killer and she had just let him come waltzing in without so much as checking his credentials.

What kind of a mother did that make her?

"Did your mom yell at you for making the horse wear her scarves?" Axel asked the possible ax murderer.

Connor looked perfectly serious as he said, "No, she decided she didn't like those scarves anymore. She said she was happy to give them to Lightning."

They were lapping this up, Brianna realized. And this stranger was obviously very good with children.

She supposed she was overreacting, she thought. If this man was a possible ax murderer or a serial killer, chances were that he wouldn't be sitting cross-legged on her floor with her children, telling them this exaggerated story.

And besides, he *did* fix her toilet, she told herself. She strongly doubted that ax murderers went around fixing toilets for their victims just before they did away with them.

Brianna had just decided to exonerate the man in her kitchen when he suddenly looked in her direction with the softest brown eyes she'd ever seen.

For the briefest of moments, she felt something inside of her tighten in response.

"Everything all settled?" he asked her.

It took her a minute to focus on his words. "With the plumber?" she finally asked. When he nodded, she said, "Yes, I convinced him that it was a false alarm and that the toilet was running fine now. He wasn't happy, but he left." Coming closer, she stood over Connor and extended her hand. "We never got a chance to finish with our introductions. I'm Brianna Childress," she told him. "And those are my children, Axel and Ava."

"I know," he said. "At least, I know who you are. The kids I have to admit were a surprise." *In more ways than one*, he thought.

Brianna's suspicions returned. She shifted so that she stood directly in front of her children, as if to protect them. "Why do you know who I am?"

Chapter Four

Connor smiled at her, doing his best to assuage the wary look that had returned to her eyes. He didn't want her afraid of him. If she was, then getting any useful information out of her might be difficult.

"I know your name," he told her, "because I've done my homework."

"You have homework?" Axel cried, appalled. "But aren't you old?"

"Axel!" Brianna chided, upset at her four-year-old son's unfiltered response to the situation.

"Yeah!" Three-year-old Ava joined forces with her mother and got into her brother's face. "You don't tell old people they're old."

She couldn't have her children here while she was trying to deal with this stranger. "Axel, Ava, why don't you two go play with Scruffy?" Brianna said, herding the dog and the half-pint dynamic duo toward the bedroom that they shared. "*Quietly* this time."

It was obvious that both children wanted to stay and hear what this new person who had come into their house had to say, but one look at their mother's face told them that they needed to listen to her.

Looking miffed, Ava reluctantly walked out of the room. "This is all your fault," she accused her brother. "You got mommy upset."

"It is not!" Axel shouted back at his sister as he left the room.

"And they're off," Brianna sighed. She tried to remember a time when life was peaceful and couldn't. Collecting herself, she turned to face Connor. "Would you mind explaining just how I figure into your 'homework'?" she asked.

"That's easy." First order of business, he thought, was to assure Brianna that he meant her no harm. Taking out his wallet, he flipped it open to show her his credentials. "I'm a private investigator and I need to ask you a few questions if you don't mind."

"What kind of questions?" Brianna wanted to know. For the life of her, she had absolutely no clue what this was about or what she could possibly tell him. Regarding him warily, she asked, "Should I be worried?"

"Why?" He tucked his wallet back into his pocket. "Have you done something bad?" he asked, amused despite himself.

"No," she answered with a little bit too much feeling.

She couldn't remember a time when she had done anything even remotely "bad." She was too busy raising two overenergetic children and holding down miscellaneous part-time jobs trying to make ends meet to do anything even remotely bad. Or fun for that matter.

"But you're here wanting to ask me questions and I haven't got the vaguest idea why," she informed him, still eyeing him nervously.

Connor felt a little guilty for making her feel so uneasy. He quickly began to explain the situation to her. "I'm looking for some information about a job you did for Charlotte Robinson last year."

Brianna blinked. She prided herself on remembering the names of the people she dealt with but this name was definitely not familiar.

"Who?"

"Charlotte Robinson," Connor repeated a little bit louder now.

The name still meant nothing to her. Brianna shook her head. "Sorry, that name doesn't ring a bell. Maybe you have me confused with someone else," she told him.

"Maybe," he allowed, not wanting to come on too strong. But he had done his due diligence and he knew he wasn't wrong about this. "However, I don't think so," he told her politely. "This is a photo of Charlotte taken in the last six months." Connor took out his cell phone and swiped through a few pictures until he came to the one he was looking for. He held it up for Brianna to see. "Look carefully. Does she look familiar?"

She took the phone from him and studied the photograph for a moment. Shaking her head, she handed the phone back to him.

"No." When he looked disappointed, she explained.

"But that really doesn't mean anything. All my business is conducted over the phone or online. I never get to meet any of my customers. But her name definitely isn't familiar," she repeated. "Sorry."

Connor put his phone in his pocket. "How about Charlotte Prendergast?" he asked. He knew that Charlotte had a number of aliases. Maybe she had been using one of them when she'd contacted Brianna.

Again Brianna shook her head. This was turning into a waste of time for both of them and she didn't have time to waste.

"Sorry," she said again. "Now I really have to—"

But Connor wasn't ready to give up just yet. "How about Charlene Pickett?" he asked, remembering yet another alias he knew that Charlotte had used at least on one other occasion.

That got Brianna's attention. While she wanted the man to leave, she had too much integrity to lie and the name he'd just said *did* sound familiar. "Say that name again, please."

"She might have used the name Charlene Pickett," he said, watching Brianna's face for the slightest sign of recognition in case she denied knowing the woman.

But she didn't.

"That does ring a bell," Brianna acknowledged. "What's with all the different names?" she couldn't help asking. "What is this woman, some kind of spy or undercover agent?" She didn't know of any other reason why anyone would be using so many aliases. Con artists were not a part of her world and she didn't do business with them.

Connor laughed dryly. "Nothing nearly that glamorous or interesting," he assured her. And then he grew more serious. He was following bread crumbs, doing his best to follow the trail left behind by the woman he felt was responsible for everything that had befallen his family. "Just what was the nature of your business with her?"

Brianna shrugged, completely at a loss as to what was going on and what it had to do with her and her family. "Charlene told me that she was putting together a genealogy chart for the Fortune family. She also asked if I could find addresses—and possible aliases— for certain people she'd uncovered in the family tree."

Connor never took his eyes off Brianna's, doing his best not to allow himself to be mesmerized by the soft brown orbs. He was onto something and couldn't afford to be distracted.

"And did you?"

"Yes, I did," she answered. "My turn," Brianna declared, catching him off guard. "Why do you want to know all this?"

Connor paused for a moment, weighing his options. He decided that sticking as close to the truth as possible would be useful in this case.

"I'm a Fortune myself, related to them," he clarified. "In all probability, one of those people she had you looking for might have been me."

Brianna's eyes widened even as she exhaled. Now it was all beginning to make sense to her.

Connor Fortunado.

Connor Fortune.

The man standing before her wasn't a potential ax

murderer. He was a man who was looking for his family, or at least parts of his family.

Brianna caught herself smiling. There was nothing sinister in that.

Reassured, Brianna relaxed. "I'm afraid I'm not going to be much help to you. I haven't heard from Charlene, or whoever she really is, in months. As a matter of fact," she said ruefully, "she still owes me money. She paid half up front and she said that she'd pay me the rest when I gave her the information.

"It took a little doing, but I managed to find some of the people she was looking for. I sent the information on to her, but…" Her voice trailed off as she looked at him, embarrassed at her naivete. "I'm still waiting for the rest of the payment."

Connor nodded. "That definitely sounds like Charlotte, all right." And then, under his breath, he murmured, "She doesn't care who she sticks it to."

He looked around the living room. There were toys, mostly very used-looking ones, scattered all over the floor. The furniture, what there was of it, was pretty threadbare.

Brianna pressed her lips together, trying not to wince as she saw him take everything in. She didn't have to be a mind reader to guess what he was thinking.

This shouldn't have happened to this woman, Connor thought. He found himself feeling guilty that she had been used like this.

"If I can track down Charlene—Charlotte—" he corrected, "maybe I can get your money for you. How much did she wind up owing you?"

Brianna didn't even have to pause to try to remember the sum. She had a good head for figures and this one was etched into her mind. "Three thousand dollars."

"Three thousand dollars," he repeated. Growing quiet for a moment, he seemed to be thinking something over. And then he said, "You said that you located those people for her?"

Where was the man going with this? she wondered. "Most of them, yes."

"Tell you what," Connor proposed. "If you can help me find Charlotte, I'll pay you that three thousand dollars she owes you—and a fee for helping me locate her on top of that. Do we have a deal?" he asked, ready to shake on it.

She wanted her money, but she was still cautious. Brianna had no intentions of entering into any agreement blindly.

"Just exactly what do you need me to do?" Brianna asked. And then, as he opened his mouth, she quickly issued her disclaimer. "Before you answer, I have to tell you right off the bat that I can't travel anywhere. I have Ava and Axel to take care of, not to mention the various furry creatures that seemed to have adopted us. And, because this job doesn't exactly provide a steady salary, I have a couple of part-time jobs to help make ends meet. I can't just abandon them."

The woman definitely came with strings, Connor thought.

"What kind of jobs?" he wanted to know, curious.

"I'm a medical transcriber and I fill in at the animal shelter reception desk a few times a week," she told him. As she said it, she was sure that any one of these things would be a deal breaker.

"Animal shelter," he repeated. "That would explain the menagerie," Connor commented.

"I've always loved animals," she told him a little defensively. She took a breath, resigning herself to the conclusion he'd undoubtedly reached. "So I guess it's a no regarding our working together."

"What makes you think that?" Connor asked, surprised. Just then, there was another crash, followed by a very plaintive "Oh-oh" coming from the room where her children had retreated. Connor couldn't help grinning. "I can come back at a more convenient time," he told her, rising to his feet.

"That would be in another fifteen years when they're both in college, provided I can keep them alive that long," Brianna commented, struggling not to be overwhelmed again. She'd lost count how many times that made in the last week.

Connor smiled at her. "I've got a feeling you can." He saw the skeptical look on her face and knew it didn't have anything to do with his last comment. She was worried about his coming back. Obviously he hadn't laid all her fears to rest. "All I want to do is pick your brain, Brianna," he told her sincerely. "I want to go over all the names that Charlotte asked you to investigate and I also want to know just what information you discovered for her."

The skeptical look was still on her flawless face. "And that's worth three thousand dollars to you?" she asked in disbelief. Something just wasn't adding up in her estimation. There had to be something more going on that she wasn't privy to.

"That is worth *everything* to me," Connor answered in all sincerity.

Brianna waited for him to elaborate, but Connor didn't say anything more on the subject.

She frowned. She didn't like getting into something without having all the cards laid out on the table, especially when she had a gut feeling that there was something more going on.

But there was no denying the fact that she could really use the money and she had a feeling that she was never going to see that money from Charlene or Charlotte or whatever the woman's real name was. This was going to be her only chance of recouping her loss.

"So, do we have a deal?" Connor asked her again, this time putting his hand out.

Common sense told her that she needed more blanks filled in, but the bills that were piling up on her desk weren't going to be paid with common sense.

Brianna put her hand into his and shook it, praying she wasn't going to regret this. "We have a deal," she told him.

"Great." A hair-raising scream came from the kids' bedroom. "You need help with that?" he asked, nodding in the direction the scream came from.

"I can handle it." Brianna looked toward the front door. "I'll just walk you out first."

He was going to tell her that he could see himself out. But there was something about this unconsciously sexy lady that told him Brianna had trust issues and he had already pushed things about as far as he thought he could for now.

So he flashed a smile at her and said, "Then I'll walk fast so you can get to your emergency."

"No emergency," she told him with just a touch of weariness as she led the way. "Just business as usual." Reaching the front door, she asked, "Is it wrong for me to hope that the next fifteen years will fly by?"

Connor laughed. "Given the situation," he answered, "there would be something wrong with you if you didn't. At least once in a while," he added, sensing that the woman really loved these two whirling dervishes that were disguised as her children. "I'll give you a call soon so we can set a time to get started," he told her.

"You have my number?" she asked, wanting to be sure he did.

"Oh yes."

The way he said that caused her stomach to tighten. She was reading into it, she silently insisted. Stiffening slightly, she said, "Goodbye."

Before Connor could respond in kind, he found himself looking at the door. She had closed it on him in one fluid motion.

He could hear her running toward the back of the house and her children. Connor shook his head. How did she manage to keep on going day after day, faced with these mini explosions? The woman definitely had her work cut out for her. Where did she find the time to get anything else done, he marveled, turning away. Her kids seemed to take up every single moment of the day as well as suck up all the oxygen in any room they were in.

Connor walked back to his car at the curb and got in. If he listened, he could still make out the sound of high voices talking over one another. This sort of thing just reinforced his feelings about the single life. The thought of coming home to that kind of chaos night after night sent a cold shiver up and down his spine.

Starting up his car, he thought of what Brianna had said about not being able to travel because of her children and their pets.

Hell, he couldn't imagine a life like that. Not being able to travel, being restricted like that because he had to be there day after day for two little warring people who had no idea of how much was being sacrificed for them.

He thought of Ava and Axel. He had to admit that he'd gotten a kick out of how they seemed to hang on his words when he told them about Lightning, but hell, he could get the same sort of attentive effect from one of his friends if he just bribed them with a couple of drinks at a restaurant.

This Brianna woman probably didn't even realize all the freedom she was missing out on, all the freedom she had given up just to put up with those two walking accidents-waiting-to-happen. He hadn't seen any evidence, such as photographs, of a husband on the scene. Nor was she wearing a wedding ring. Was the woman tackling all this by herself? She had to be a little crazy to do that.

Yes sir, Connor thought, he was really glad he wasn't in a committed relationship. Heaven forbid some cute little number started having designs on him, making wedding plans in her head.

Wedding rings reminded him much too much of nooses and he wasn't about to slip one of those around his neck, no way. While he could see, he supposed, his brothers and sisters settling down into what they were hoping were lives of domestic bliss, he had just been exposed to a *real* picture of what happened after the words "I do" were spoken.

In very short order "I do" turned into "I don't" as those words applied to doing things, taking off at a moment's notice, having fun. All of that fell by the wayside, a casualty in the wake of deluded dreams of happiness.

That kind of happiness was just a myth. *Real* happiness was something that the individual made happen. The individual, not the couple, Connor silently underscored as he drove back to his parents' home.

No, if he was ever tempted to go the route that his siblings had all opted to tread, he hoped that someone would have the good sense to shoot him—or at least tie him up until the moment of insanity passed and he was back to himself again.

Connor turned up the music and tried, just for the next half hour, to clear his brain of everything.

It was easier said than done. For some reason, images of Ava and Axel insisted on flashing through his mind's eye.

Along with that of their mother.

He turned the music up even louder.

Chapter Five

Brianna didn't have time to think about the unsettling stranger she had just sent on his way. She had a volatile situation she needed to defuse. The shouting was getting louder.

Moving quickly, she headed toward the children's bedroom.

When she got there, she saw that Axel and Ava were at each other's throats, fighting for sole possession of a one-eared stuffed rabbit. Getting between them, she managed to separate her children—and save the rabbit.

"Okay, you two, you need a time-out," she told them sternly. Physically holding them apart, she informed her children, "I'm going to separate you so you can think about how you're supposed to behave." Brianna gave her noisy twosome a dark look. "Especially when we have company."

Axel looked up at his mother, puzzled. "What company?"

"*Any* company," Brianna emphasized. Axel was just pretending not to understand. He was brighter than that, she thought.

"She means the man," Ava told her brother in her superior voice. And then a thought seemed to occur to her. She turned toward her mother, distressed. "Is he mad at Axel?"

Judging by the look on her daughter's face, Brianna guessed that Ava was harboring a crush on Connor Fortunado. *Wonderful*, Brianna thought. Just what she needed.

"No, Ava, Mr. Fortunado is not 'mad' at Axel. I'm sure he understands that sometimes children need to be reminded how to behave around people," Brianna told the battling duo.

"Can I be around him?" Ava asked hopefully.

Brianna wasn't sure what her daughter was asking. It was hard to second-guess what was in either of her children's heads.

"What?"

"You said you were sep-per-ating us," Ava answered, carefully enunciating the word that was giving her tongue trouble. "So I want you to put me in his room. Mr. Fortu—what you said," she concluded, unable to say Connor's last name.

Not waiting for permission, Ava darted out of the room she shared with her brother and ran back to the living room.

"Ava Susan Childress, you come back here," Brianna called after her daughter. Ava's escape had caught her completely off guard.

"You're in trouble now," Axel declared gleefully, running in after his sister. "Mama called out all your names."

Ava had reached the living room. Surprised to find it empty, she looked around with a puzzled expression on her face. When she heard her mother and brother coming in behind her, she spun around to face them.

"Where is he, Mama?" Ava asked, disappointed. "Where's the man?"

Brianna tried not to focus on her daughter's disobedience. Instead, she tried to remember what it was like to be Ava's age.

"He went home, Ava," she told her daughter.

Distressed, Ava whirled around to glare at her brother. "He went away because you made his feelings hurt."

"No, I didn't!" Axel protested, growing defensive again. It seemed to be his default state.

Ava had turned her attention toward her mother, the woman who could fix anything.

"Make him come back, Mama. I liked him. He has a horse he puts clothes on," Ava said as if that was what made the man so special to her. "I wanted to see the horse."

"Come here," Brianna coaxed.

She took each of her children by the hand and led them to the sofa. Sitting down, she tugged each of their hands to get them to sit down on either side of her. Their upturned faces made her think of tulips seeking out the sun.

"Listen to me, you two. I am thrilled you have such a zest for life, I really am. But just for now, could you try to be a little less...zesty?" she asked, looking from one small upturned face to the other. "You're wearing me out."

"Wearing you out where?" Axel wanted to know, looking all over his mother. He was obviously taking what she'd said literally.

Ava frowned disdainfully at her brother. "She means she's tired, dummy."

"Oh." Axel sat up a little straighter, apparently feeling he had the solution. "Go lie down, Mommy," he urged with a smile.

There was no way she was doing that and leaving her two hellions to their own devices.

"Heaven forbid. By the time I got up again, I wouldn't have a house standing," she murmured under her breath. "Besides, I don't want to lie down," she told her children, slipping an arm around each of their shoulders. "What I want is for you two to *calm* down. Do you think you can do that for me?"

Both Axel and Ava solemnly bobbed their heads up and down.

Brianna didn't believe they meant it for a minute, but at least she had them pausing for a moment, allowing her to catch her breath.

"Is he coming back?" Ava asked in a smaller, hesitant voice.

"You mean Mr. Fortunado?" Brianna asked.

Axel giggled, then covered his mouth. The giggle only grew louder. "That's a funny name."

"Yes, it is," Brianna agreed. "And yes, Ava, he's coming back."

Ava's eyes widened and practically sparkled. "When?" she asked eagerly.

"I'm not sure yet." Brianna scrutinized her daughter's face. She had never known either of her children to take to an adult this quickly before. "You liked him, didn't you?" she asked her daughter.

Ava looked shy for a moment, and then almost blushed. "Uh-huh."

Curious why she was so taken with the man, Brianna asked her daughter, "Why?"

"'Cause he told us a story. And he smiled nice," Ava added very seriously.

She was going to have to watch this one, Brianna thought. Her daughter was obviously skipping right over the "boys are icky" stage, going straight to being a tiny, budding femme fatale.

Not to be left out, Axel added his two cents about the stranger who had been in their house. "And *he* didn't tell us to be quiet."

"Well, if you calm down a little once in a while I wouldn't have to tell you that so often, either," Brianna pointed out.

Axel hung his head as if he had suddenly become contrite and in a very small voice said to her, "Okay, Mommy."

"Okay, Mama," Ava added, not to be outdone by her brother.

Brianna sighed quietly. This docile moment had a life expectancy of about a minute and a half, but it was nice while it lasted and she intended to enjoy it until Axel and Ava returned to their natural, rambunctious behavior.

Kissing both of their heads one at a time, Brianna

rose from the sofa. "See how long you can be good," she requested.

"I can be gooder than Axel," Ava assured her boastfully.

Small light eyebrows drew together forming an annoyed, wavy line that joined together above Axel's sprinkling of freckles.

"No, you can't," he informed his sister. "I'm gooder than you."

"You're *both* equally as good," Brianna told him, raising her voice to stop the argument before it could take off.

Today was going to be a very long, long day, Brianna thought.

Leaving her pint-size warriors, she walked into the small room she used as an office. There was barely enough room there for her desk and chair. Directly in the corner she had a set of plastic drawers she'd bought at the local membership store. She kept all her files in those drawers, packed away.

She wasn't looking forward to the task ahead of her, but she needed to get started. She intended to find her notes outlining what she had sent to this person Fortunado was looking for.

She knew she had sent the last correspondence to the woman approximately three months ago. Brianna remembered that it had taken her more than a bit of searching before she tracked down a large number of the people the woman told her she was trying to find.

Brianna recalled thinking that the request was a little strange. Her client had told her it was for a genealogy chart but the people she was trying to find all seemed to be around the same age.

At the time she decided that it was none of her business. She didn't care that much *why* the woman was looking to find these people as long as the woman was willing to pay money for the results.

Apparently, though, this Charlene/Charlotte person wasn't willing to make good on her promise. When Brianna hadn't heard anything from her client, she'd tried to contact her and request payment. But the letter had been returned, stamped Unable to Deliver, Return to Sender.

At the time, she'd been too busy to try to follow up and find Charlene's whereabouts. And then both of her kids came down with really bad colds that they kept passing to each other, so she had no time to track the woman down. Stressed, she'd given up, deciding to philosophically chalk it up to just one of those things—and then Fortunado had turned up on her doorstep.

She caught herself wondering what he must have thought when she opened the door and grabbed his hand, dragging him into her bathroom and pointing to the almost-overflowing, nonfunctioning toilet.

Brianna laughed to herself as she began to look through her files. You just never knew how things were going to turn out, she mused. Maybe she'd actually see that three thousand dollars after all.

At least she had hope.

"You have a lead?" Valene asked, staring at her older brother uncertainly. The moment she had seen Connor pull up to the house, she had all but waylaid him at the door.

"What are you doing here?" he asked, surprised to see her. After all, she hadn't lived on the family estate for a while now.

She gave him a look that all but said he was being a typical male. "Wedding plans, remember?" she reminded him.

That made him a little confused. "I thought that was yesterday."

Val rolled her eyes. "Could you *be* more of a man?" she asked, referring to his cluelessness as to what it took to pull together a wedding.

"That depends. What's in it for me?" he teased her with a grin and a wink.

Valene blew out a breath. "Can the charming stuff. I'm talking about how clueless you are when it comes to planning a wedding."

He saw no point in arguing her assessment. "And I intend to blissfully remain that way for the rest of my life."

"Really?" she questioned, giving him an evil eye, unwilling to believe he was actually serious. "You actually plan on remaining alone for the rest of your life?"

A twinkle came into Connor's eyes as his grin grew wider. "I didn't say that," he pointed out.

Valene sighed mightily, exasperated. Oh well, Connor would change his mind when the right woman came along, she thought. "Getting back to what I asked before you started to give me your unwanted opinion about weddings, do you have a lead? So soon?"

"What makes you say I have a lead?" he wanted to know.

He had left early this morning in order not to say anything to anyone. He'd wanted to find out if he could get anything from the freelancer first. There was no point in raising people's hopes for no reason.

"Mom said you took off really early this morning. I assumed that meant that you might be onto something," Val explained.

"Right now what I have is a lead on a lead," Connor told his sister.

Val frowned slightly, confused. "What's that supposed to mean?"

He debated keeping his own counsel for a minute, then decided there was no harm in sharing what he'd been doing. "It means that I found someone who did some research for good old Charlotte—"

Questions immediately filled his sister's head. "What kind of research?"

"Do you remember that binder Charlotte was supposed to have compiled on all of Gerald's offspring?" he asked.

"Yes?"

Valene stretched out the word, as if afraid of where this was going. She remembered talk of a binder. She also remembered thinking that Charlotte was really strange to take the time to carefully put together all that miscellaneous information. To her it was like deliberately rubbing salt into her wounds since the names represented all of her husband's infidelities.

"Well, it now looks like she was trying to locate the whereabouts of as many of her former husband's progeny as possible," Connor said.

Valene shook her head, mystified. "Why would she go through all that trouble?"

"Well," Connor said thoughtfully, having pondered the matter on his drive home, "if I was to make a guess, I'd say she was trying to locate them so that she could hurt them."

Valene's first reaction was to dismiss what her brother had said. "Even she's not that evil."

That wasn't the way Connor saw it. "Would you like to make a bet on that?"

His sister shook her head, feeling dismayed. "No," she answered. Charlotte Robinson was the very definition of evil. "You know, Gerald is a soulless alley cat, but Charlotte's no prize, either. If you ask me, those two royally deserve each other. Someone should take both of them, lock them in a room and throw away the key. Forever."

Connor laughed dryly. "I'm certainly not arguing that, but it's way too late in my opinion. They've already done a lot of damage, both in their own way."

"So," Valene said, returning to the subject, "what are you planning on doing with this lead to a lead?"

He'd outlined that in his mind on the way home, as well. "First thing is to see if I can find out just who Charlotte had this woman—"

"It's a woman?" Valene interrupted, realizing she had no idea exactly who her brother had gone to look up.

"Yes, Brianna Childress is most definitely a woman," he answered. "I'm going to see if she can give me the names and address—"

Valene interrupted again. "A pretty woman?" she wanted to know.

She'd picked up a vibe from her brother and wondered if there was something more to his interaction with this Brianna than he was telling. His response that Brianna was "most definitely a woman" had Valene thinking.

Valene's question out of left field made him come to a skidding halt again. Connor frowned at what he considered a pointless question.

"What difference does that make?" he asked.

Val smiled at her supposedly perpetual playboy brother. She was pretty sure she saw beneath that act of his. "You tell me."

"I haven't got the slightest idea what you're talking about," he said, exasperated. "All this wedding planning that you're talking about all the time has obviously fried your brain."

Valene merely smiled at him as if she knew something that he didn't. Not about to get distracted, Connor decided to just ignore his sister.

"You were saying about getting the names and addresses…?" Her voice trailed off as she indicated to her brother that she was waiting for him to continue what he had been saying.

"Since we don't know who Charlene was looking for, getting those names and addresses might help me get in touch with these people so I can warn them that Charlotte might be out to get them."

Valene frowned. She completely agreed with her brother's intentions, but she had a feeling he was going to have some trouble convincing people he was on the level.

She looked at him dubiously. "That doesn't sound crazy at all, does it?" she asked sarcastically.

"Well, whether it sounds crazy or not, I have to try to reach these people. Now that we agree Charlotte's most likely behind some if not all of the things that have been going on, I don't want to have these people on my conscience.

"Besides," Connor continued with a grin, "you forget, little sister. I can be very convincing when I put my mind to it."

"No," Valene replied. "I haven't forgotten. I just hope, if you're right about this—" and she had a feeling he was "—that it's not too late."

Connor grew serious. "You're not the only one," he assured her.

Chapter Six

She hadn't expected to hear from Connor Fortunado so soon.

When the landline in her office rang the following morning, Brianna thought it was either someone calling to make use of her research service—or some anonymous person conducting a survey. It seemed like these days there was always someone conducting a survey and she would have loved to just let the call go to her answering machine, but because of the business she was in, she couldn't afford to miss even one potential client.

The moment she picked up the receiver and heard the deep voice on the other end, even though she'd never received a call from him before, Brianna knew who the caller was. She recognized Connor's voice the moment she heard him say, "Hello."

Even though yesterday had turned out to be an even more hectic day than usual—she had transcribing to catch up on and then she got a last-minute call to fill in at the animal shelter—images of the tall, hazel-eyed private investigator kept popping up in her head when she least expected them. For some reason that she couldn't even begin to understand, she felt like there was a connection between them, though for the life of her she couldn't explain why.

"Ms. Childress?" the baritone voice asked, rumbling against her ear. "This is Connor Fortunado. We met yesterday."

Did Fortunado think that dealing with her children had wiped out her memory? "Yes, I know who this is," she replied.

"You were expecting my call," Connor guessed, thinking that was why she was able to recognize his voice so quickly.

"Actually, I wasn't," Brianna admitted. No, she thought, that was a lie. She'd been hoping he'd call. After all, he had said he'd be in touch. "At least, not this soon," she amended.

"You're busy," he surmised, judging from the unsettled note in her voice. That, and the woman obviously had her hands full dealing with her children. He could hear their voices shouting in the background. "I got you at a bad time."

"No, no, I'm not busy," Brianna assured him quickly. Maybe a little too quickly, she realized. She tempered her answer. "I mean, no more than usual."

The next second she winced as Ava's and Axel's voices grew louder, arguing over the board game they were playing. She'd given them a classic game—Chutes and Ladders—in hopes that it would keep them busy for a while. Busy and quiet. Apparently that had been too much to hope for.

Connor chuckled. "I hear your kids," he commented. He'd meant it as an icebreaker, nothing more.

Brianna sighed. She knew that her children were going to outgrow this stage, but when? "Everyone hears my kids."

He laughed out loud. The woman apparently still had a sense of humor despite everything. Since he'd called her, he decided to ask, thinking he had nothing to lose, "Do you have any time today to get together for a couple of hours?"

"I have time," she answered with feeling. "My schedule is chaotic, but flexible. What time would you like to come over?"

He thought for a second, trying to decide what might be best for the woman. "How does one o'clock sound?"

Brianna thought for a moment. "Right after lunch and before the second wave of insanity starts," she pronounced. "Sounds fine."

"Good. Then I'll be there at one," Connor agreed, glad that was settled.

"I'll be here," she assured him. As she hung up the receiver, placing it back in the cradle, she murmured, "I'm always here."

For the most part, Brianna had made her peace with being a homebody several years ago. But she had to admit there were times when she wished that her life was about something more than juggling three jobs, two children and a varying, ever-growing number of cats and dogs.

Not that she minded all that, she quickly amended, but every once in a while, she caught herself thinking that it would be nice to have something else to look forward to. To occasionally have someone around who appreciated how she never dropped any of the proverbial balls she was perpetually juggling.

"This is no time to feel sorry for yourself," Brianna lectured herself, exasperated with this momentary lapse on her part. "You're doing just fine."

There'd been a time when she was certain that she wouldn't be. That she was just going to fall apart in little pieces. That had been just after Jonny walked out and left her.

Left *them*, she corrected because the man she had devoted herself to had walked out not just on her but on Axel and Ava, as well.

His children.

After several years of putting off taking that "big step" as he had always referred to marriage, Jonny decided that not only wasn't he cut out to be a husband, he didn't *want* to be a father, either. After years of being there for him, bending her life around the man, she'd been devastated when Jonny made it very clear that he didn't want to be there for her.

A substance abuser who had never really kicked the habit despite all his promises to "clean up his act," he wound up choosing his habit over her and left.

She and Jonny had been a dysfunctional unit, but being without him was worse.

At least at first.

But she couldn't fall to pieces, Brianna had told herself fiercely. She'd had an eighteen-month-old and three-month-old depending on her and *only* her. So she'd forced herself to put one foot in front of the other and somehow she'd got through one day, then another and another until somehow a whole month had passed. And then six months.

Somehow, she'd just kept going, setting her sights on making it through another month.

She'd had no longer-range plans than that. All she wanted to do was get to the end of the month.

Each month.

And she had. In fact, she'd made it three years.

Rousing herself, Brianna blocked out any more thoughts that fell outside of the parameters of the project she was currently working on. She just focused on that.

For once, there were no bloodcurdling screams coming from anywhere in the house to distract her. The noise level had lowered to a familiar, almost-comforting hum.

Brianna started to work, knowing this peace wouldn't last long.

It was too quiet. In the last twenty minutes she hadn't heard any crashes, any yelling or even the sound of scuffling that occasionally came from the wrestling matches that Axel and Ava sporadically engaged in.

Had they run away? Or worse, done something to each other simultaneously so that neither one was able to cry out?

Uneasy now, she knew her imagination was running

away with her. She didn't usually break for lunch until twelve but even though it was just eleven thirty, she stopped and went in search of the twosome.

Maybe they had both come down with something, she thought, trying to find a reason why she wasn't hearing *anything*. Nothing short of a sudden mutual illness could render them this quiet for this long.

Walking into the living room, Brianna was both relieved and somewhat concerned to find her children watching one of the cable channels. As she drew closer she saw that they were both sitting on the floor, mesmerized by a lion stalking his prey, in this case a helpless zebra.

She knew how this story ended and she didn't want them to see it.

Moving swiftly, Brianna got in front of the TV monitor and changed the channel. She pressed the numbers and the picture on the screen instantly changed from a stalking lion to a cartoon rabbit getting the better of a determined, if inept hunter.

That was more like it, Brianna thought with satisfaction.

"Mom!" Axel lamented indignantly, "The lion was just about to get that striped horse!"

"No, he wasn't," Ava insisted. Her arm was draped over Scruffy, trapping the dog against her. Scruffy was used to this and didn't seem to mind, Brianna noted. "The horsie was going to get away," she informed her brother with the kind of confidence reserved only for the very young and innocent.

And they're back, Brianna thought.

"You want lunch in the kitchen or in front of the TV?" she asked.

Once, in her younger, prechildren days, she had come up with all sorts of rules she was going to make her future, unborn children follow. They were going to do chores and only be allowed to watch one hour of TV programming a week.

All that had fallen by the wayside rather quickly when she was faced with the reality of actually *living* with children and making it all work. Especially as a single mother.

"In front of the TV!" both children cried out in unison.

Finally, she thought, they had found something to agree on. It didn't happen that often.

"Okay," she told them, "but you have to promise not to argue."

"I'll be good, Mom. I won't argue," Axel promised, slanting a look at Ava. The look he'd flashed implied that he thought his sister would.

Ava was quick to pick up on the implied insult. "No, *I* won't argue," she declared with feeling.

Any mother could read between the lines, especially when those lines were two feet high the way they were here. It was only a matter of time before the next argument would break out.

But she pretended, for the time being, to believe them.

"Good," Brianna said with finality, "you both won't argue. Try to remember that," she cautioned her children as she turned around and went into the kitchen to prepare their lunches.

* * *

Brianna had just collected the empty dishes and put them into the sink when she heard Ava—Ava moved with a light step, while Axel seemed to stomp whenever he hurried—rush across the room.

Since nothing had crashed or fallen, Brianna didn't think anything of her daughter's sudden mobility until she heard Ava calling out excitedly.

"He's back, Mama! He came back. I see him outside the house!"

"Who came back?" Axel wanted to know.

The next second, not to be left out, the little boy made tracks to the window so he could see whatever it was that his sister saw.

"He did. The man," Ava cried happily, pointing out the window.

Brianna realized what was going on and who her daughter was so excited about.

Grabbing a dish towel, Brianna dried her hands and hurried into the living room. Before she could reach either of her children, she saw that Ava was already at the door, just about to open it.

"Ava! What did I tell you about opening the door?" Brianna cried loud enough to freeze the little girl in her tracks.

"Not to do it?" It wasn't a statement, it was more of a guess.

"Then why are you opening it?" Brianna wanted to know. Reaching her daughter, she put her hand over the doorknob and removed Ava's hand, preventing the little girl from throwing the door open.

Ava looked up at her, totally mystified.

"'Cause it's him," she answered as if she couldn't understand why her mother was even asking her that question. "The man from yesterday. The man who put clothes on his horsie," Ava added for good measure just in case her mother still didn't know who she was talking about.

"That doesn't matter," Brianna told Ava sternly. "You don't ever, ever open the door, understand?" she warned her daughter.

Light eyebrows scrunched up, disappearing beneath dark brown bangs.

"Ever?" Ava repeated. "Not even when I'm going to school?" she asked. "How're we gonna get out of the rooms?"

"We can't get out if we can't open the door," Axel complained, chiming in. For once he actually appeared to be on Ava's side.

They were just too smart for their own good, Brianna thought wearily. They were certainly too smart for *her* own good.

"We'll talk about that when the time comes," Brianna told her daughter, doing her best not to lose her temper right now.

The doorbell rang.

Ava looked at her mother, the lecture forgotten as excitement filled her at the prospect of seeing her mother's friend again.

"It's him!" she cried. Ava tugged on her mother's arm to motivate her. "Open it, Mama. Open it before he goes away!"

Any hope Brianna had that yesterday had been a

fluke evaporated. She knew better now. Ava definitely had a crush on the private investigator.

She was going to have to address that before it got out of hand, Brianna thought.

But obviously not now.

Shooing Ava away from the door, she opened it to admit Connor, doing her best to keep her composure.

He smiled at Brianna, then immediately saw that she wasn't alone. "Hi, I see you brought your welcoming committee," he observed.

"No, no commit-tee. It's just me," Ava told him. "Ava," she said, in case he had forgotten her name. She preened a little as she said it.

"And me," Axel said.

"And they were just going out to play in the backyard," Brianna assured him, ushering her children toward the rear of the house and the sliding glass door that led into the fenced yard.

"No, we weren't," Ava protested, speaking up. She moved a little closer to Connor. "We were going to stay right here," she said, looking up at him with a big, sunny smile.

Okay, this had gone on long enough. "Axel, Ava, backyard. Now," Brianna ordered.

Long faces greeted her order. Seeing that their mother meant business, very slowly they shuffled their feet all the way to the sliding glass door, and then went out into the backyard. It was very clearly under protest.

Connor watched them go along with their mother, who kept a watchful eye on their reluctant exodus. He couldn't help grinning at the pint-size dramatics.

Satisfied that they had gone out the way they had

been told to, Brianna finally turned around to face her guest.

"Was it just my imagination, or was Ava flirting with me?" Connor asked her mother.

He was accustomed to being flirted with, but the person doing the flirting was usually at least old enough to vote. This time the person flirting with him wasn't even old enough to attend kindergarten.

"I'm going to have a problem with that girl," Brianna said, answering his question indirectly. "Ava's never done that before, although that's not saying much since she's only three," she was quick to add. Brianna shook her head, at a loss how to effectively handle this. "Before I had kids, I used to think I had all the answers. Now even my questions have questions. It seems like every day there's something new to deal with," she said with a sigh.

"What does her dad say?" Connor asked.

The question had come out automatically and the moment he said it, he found himself regretting it. He hadn't meant to get so personal.

Brianna shrugged as she led the way to her office. "Nothing as far as I know."

Connor read between the lines. Then, to make sure, he glanced at her left hand. Still no wedding ring. She hadn't forgotten it, she didn't have one, he thought. "You're doing this on your own?"

She thought that was obvious. "Can't you tell?" she asked ruefully.

His tone was serious as he answered the question. "Not really."

That surprised her. She'd gotten the impression that

the man was on top of things. "You're kidding." Reassessing the situation, she decided that Connor Fortunado was just being polite.

He looked at her and said in all seriousness, "No. I just see a couple of happy, spirited kids. Nothing to indicate that there's no dad in the picture."

"Spirited," Brianna repeated, amused at the private investigator's choice of words. "Oh, those two are spirited all right. They're spirited from sunup to sundown and longer. One thing those two don't run out of is spirit. Sometimes I really wish they had less of it."

But he had a feeling he knew better. "No, you don't," Connor said.

His comment surprised her. "Oh? Why's that?"

Connor smiled at her, stepping back so that she entered her office first. It was the kind of smile that told her he wasn't fooled by what she'd just stated.

"Because spirited kids become the people who turn their dreams into reality."

He said it with such certainty, she found herself really wanting to believe him.

Chapter Seven

Brianna's eyes met his and she smiled gratefully at the private investigator. "I think I really needed to hear that," she told Connor. "That was a very nice thing for you to say." She gave him a way out. "Even if you didn't mean it."

"Oh, but I did," he said. "I was pretty much a hellion when I was a kid. You can ask any of my sisters— they'll tell you," he added as verification. "Even so, things turned out pretty well for me. I got to follow my passion."

His disarming smile seemed to burrow right into her. Brianna blinked, rousing herself.

"You have sisters?" she asked Connor, trying to envision the tall, handsome man before her as a rebellious little boy. There was a glint in his eye, but she still couldn't see him that way.

"That I do," he assured her. There was no missing the fond note in his voice.

"How many?" she wanted to know. She couldn't deny that the idea of being part of a large family had always intrigued her. It was something that she had always wished for and never had.

"Three," he answered. Seeing that he had caught her interest and wanting to cultivate that interest so that she felt more at ease with him and more inclined to be forthcoming, he added, "I've got two brothers, as well."

Having grown up alone, she could hardly visualize being part of such a large family. She found herself envying him. "Wow, that *is* a full house."

He laughed softly. "I'm sure my mother would agree with you." Since Brianna seemed so interested in his family dynamics, he felt it only fair to return the favor. "How many siblings do you have?"

Her smile struck him as sad when she answered his question. "None."

"Oh." There was a moment of awkwardness because of the sad tone he'd detected in her voice, but then he found a way to turn the situation around. "That means you got to be the center of your parents' attention."

Her sad smile seemed to intensify. "You have a nice way of saying things," she told him, "but no, that wasn't the case." Clearing her throat, Brianna changed the subject. "I went through my files after you left and found most of my correspondence with that woman you were asking about yesterday."

"Charlotte," Connor said, supplying his step-aunt's name.

"Charlotte," Brianna repeated, confirming that was

who she'd meant. "Although she did sign all her email Charlene Pickett," she reminded him, "so don't let that confuse you." Brianna paused for a second, debating whether she should ask, then decided he could always just beg off giving her an honest answer. He'd been vague yesterday. "Why the need for different names?" she wanted to know. "Is she wanted by the law or something like that?"

"She should be." The answer came out without any thought and for now, it was all he allowed himself to say on the subject. Once he found a way to definitely prove that Charlotte was behind all the things that had been going on, he was confident that Charlotte Prendergast Robinson—or whatever she chose to call herself—was going to be languishing in a prison cell for a very long, long time.

When he didn't say anything further, Brianna continued with what she had been saying to him. "Well, I haven't finished going through everything—sometimes my filing system gets away from me," she confessed, embarrassed. "There might be a couple more names that she wanted me to look into, but I did find most of them," she told Connor.

Brianna placed a bunch of folders on the desk in front of him.

Picking them up, Connor quickly reviewed the names that were written on the side of each of the folders. Some were familiar, many weren't. "You found these people for her?" This would make finding these people easier for him.

The smile on her face was a bit rueful. "Again, I did manage to track down most of them." She paused, deciding to be more specific in her answer. "Eleven of these people, to be exact. I told her I'd get back to her when I found where the others were." She shrugged, hating that the situation had gotten away from her. She was accustomed to being more in control than this. "But since she didn't get back to me with at least another partial payment, I was forced to just let the matter drop."

"But you did manage to locate eleven of these people?" he asked, wanting to be clear.

"I recall a twelfth person," she said now, remembering another name. "But that last one isn't in these files. I checked," she told him. "It has to be somewhere in the rest of the folders."

Connor looked down at the folders she had handed him, then raised his eyes to hers. "And these aren't in your computer?" he questioned incredulously.

She'd been on the receiving end of that look more than once. She admitted that in this day and age, it was hard for people to understand why she'd choose to keep handwritten notes instead of storing everything on a laptop or a tablet.

"I prefer to hold paper in my hand," she said. Then, not giving him an opportunity to comment, she quickly said, "I know, I know, you probably think I'm incredibly old-fashioned. Well, you're right," she confessed. There was no point in pretending otherwise. "I am."

"Actually, I wasn't thinking that at all," Connor replied. "What I was thinking was that I kind of thought that was charming."

Charming. The word replayed itself in her head. She hadn't seen that coming.

"Well, that's the first time I've ever heard it referred to as that," Brianna admitted. She rather liked hearing him say that. "Most people think it means that I'm computer illiterate, which I'm not," she assured him quickly. "I just prefer to work this way."

"And you're perfectly entitled to your choices," he responded. "They obviously work for you."

Brianna wasn't used to being on the receiving end of compliments and she had absolutely no practice in how to respond. At a loss, she cleared her throat again.

"Yes, well, why don't you read what I came up with," she suggested, nodding at the folders he was still holding, "and I'll try to see if I can find the missing file— or files."

She really couldn't remember at this point just how many more names there were.

"Okay." Connor looked around the exceptionally small room. His parents' house had closets that were larger than this room she was apparently using as her office. "Where can I sit?" he wanted to know. From what he could see—and everything *was* out in plain sight—she just had the one desk, a pressed wood affair that looked as if she had put it together herself. There was a chair up against it that didn't match the desk.

"You can take the desk," Brianna told him. "I don't need to use it to go through the papers in my filing cabinet."

Connor looked around again, but he still didn't see anything that fit that description.

A monk's cell probably had more furnishings than this room, he thought.

"I don't see a file cabinet," he told her. "Is it in another room?"

"Not *file* cabinet," Brianna corrected. "*Filing* cabinet. It's what I call these," she said, gesturing toward the plastic drawers that she had piled on top of each other.

There were three see-through drawers all told, the type made to hold anything from toys to towels. But apparently in this particular case, they held the various notes and files that comprised her research projects.

Out of the corner of his eye, he saw her looking at him. He proceeded delicately. "You have a unique filing system," he finally commented.

At least he wasn't being critical, Brianna thought, relieved. "It works for me."

He didn't care how she had gone about doing it; he just cared about the results she had come up with. "That's all that counts, isn't it?"

Brianna studied the man in her office. Was he just trying to make her feel good, or was there a reason he was saying all these nice things to her, she wondered.

Was he trying to get her to lower her guard? Did that mean that there was some sort of an ulterior motive behind what he was saying?

What kind of an ulterior motive?

What happened to you? You used to trust people, Brianna upbraided herself.

But that had been a lifetime ago, before Jonny had walked out of her life. She'd always had a penchant for picking up strays, Jonny included. And for trying to fix things, from animals to people. But when Jonny had abruptly left, something had broken inside of her and she'd found herself second-guessing everything that happened, everything that she felt, from there on in.

Connor picked up on her mood shift. She'd grown quiet.

"Is something wrong?" he asked her, wondering if he'd said anything to set her down this path.

Brianna blinked, banishing the fog that had temporarily descended on her brain.

"What? No, no," she said with feeling, as if to deny anything he might be thinking, whatever it might be. "I was just trying to remember where I filed that missing folder or folders."

It was a lie, but it was better than going into a long explanation about her gnawing uncertainty. Besides, the man wouldn't want to hear about that. He just wanted to review her findings and glean whatever it was he was trying to find out. She knew he wasn't telling her everything. But as long as it didn't interfere with her work, that was his right.

She cleared her throat again, not realizing that he was beginning to think of that as her "tell."

"Did you mean what you said yesterday?" she asked Connor.

He had sat down at the desk and had just begun to look through the first folder. Looking her way, he said, "Refresh my memory. What did I say?"

She knew it. He was going to plead amnesia. "About paying me the three thousand dollars that Charlene Pickett was supposed to pay for the information I sent her."

He remembered that quite well. "Yes, but I also

said that payment was contingent on you helping me locate Charlotte."

Brianna nodded, recalling the whole exchange. "Yes, you did say that," she agreed. "I was just asking to see if *you* remembered."

Connor was *not* in the habit of paying off any of Charlotte Robinson's debts. Until it had come to light that Gerald Robinson was his father's half brother, he hadn't even given the woman so much as a second thought because he hadn't *known* about her or her bizarre behavior, nor about her connection to his own family.

But it was clear that Charlotte had obviously stiffed Brianna and had no intention of making good on her promise to pay. Beyond the fact that it was the wrong thing to do, this mother of two was clearly in need of every dime that had been promised to her for services rendered. He felt somewhat responsible that she had trusted Charlotte even though he'd had nothing to do with that.

That fact notwithstanding, Connor still felt he should cover the outstanding debt.

"Tell you what," Connor proposed. "Since you're obviously an honorable woman of her word, why don't I pay you the money for the work ahead of time?"

Pride reared its head and had her looking at him warily. "Why would you do that?"

Turning in the chair to face her, he spread his hands wide. "I'm just paying up front for services rendered— and to be rendered."

That was all well and good, Brianna thought. However, there was something else to consider here.

"But what if I can't find her?" she challenged.

She needed the money—she had yet to get ahead of all of her bills and possibly never would—but she had her pride. She wasn't a charity case and didn't want Fortunado to treat her as one.

"I have a feeling that you will," he told her easily. "But even if it turns out that we can't locate Charlotte because she's hidden herself in some cave, that's no reason why you shouldn't be paid for your efforts. It's only fair," he stressed.

Still, the situation disturbed her. Temptation warred with her sense of integrity. "I don't want to take advantage of you," she protested.

This woman had to be one in a million, Connor thought with admiration. He knew of a lot of people who would have jumped at the chance to take him up on his offer. For that matter, he knew of people who would be more than willing to take advantage of the situation if they could find a way to get away with it.

And here *she* was, definitely hurting for money—the woman was working three jobs for heaven sakes—and she was definitely *not* jumping at the chance to take advantage of his offer. She was even trying to talk him out of it. Who did that?

"You're not taking advantage of me if I'm the one trying to get you to accept the money," he pointed out.

Making up his mind, Connor pushed aside the folder he was reading and took out his checkbook. The desk space was limited and he needed a flat space in order to be able to write out the check.

"Do I make this out to you, or do you have a company name you'd rather I use?" he asked her, looking at her over his shoulder.

He was really going to do it, Brianna thought, amazed. He was just going to hand her the three thousand dollars whether or not she found the woman he was looking for. She knew she should try to talk him out of it, to tell him that she would wait until her part in this was done. But the truth of it was she really didn't have that luxury. She had children and bills and she could *definitely* use the three thousand dollars he was offering to pay her.

Suspicions were born in the wake of her amazement. There had to be something more, she thought. Didn't there? "And all you want me to do for this money is to help you locate this woman?" she asked.

He didn't answer her directly. "Trust me, there's no 'all' about it. If there was, I would have already done it myself." Charlotte had proven to be as slippery as the proverbial greased pig. "Like I said, you will definitely be earning your money."

She tended to believe him despite her newly acquired suspicious nature. "How long have you been looking for her?" she wanted to know, curious.

"A few weeks." Up until that point, he'd still been piecing things together. The link between the three attacks aimed at the family hadn't come to light before then, nor had the link blatantly pointing toward Charlotte.

"*Why* are you looking for her?" Brianna asked him, pinning him with a look.

She had a very compelling way about her, not to mention eyes that could induce any man to suddenly feel as if he wanted to make a full confession of any secret he might be harboring from the world.

But the fewer people who knew what was going on—until he could safely prove it—the better.

So Connor told her, "For now that's my business."

He waited for her to attempt to coax the information out of him. All the women he'd ever known were as curious as cats. However, she surprised him.

"I can respect that," she said quietly.

He waited for the other shoe to drop and for her to change her mind.

Neither happened.

"Okay, then," he said, regrouping. "You didn't answer my question. Shall I make this out to you, or to your company?"

"To the company," she told him.

"The company it is," Connor replied. With smooth, even strokes, he wrote out the check to the business he'd originally looked up, and then handed it to her.

Brianna glanced at the check out of habit, even though something told her it would be for the correct amount.

It was.

What she noticed more than the correct amount was the fluid letters that were on the check. "You have nice handwriting," she commented.

"That was my mother's doing," he admitted, giving credit where it was due. "She's not a strict woman, but there are certain things she always insisted on. One of those things was that we all had handwriting that was not just legible, but uniform. She maintained that people could tell a lot about a person by their handwriting and she wanted all of us to be held in high regard by everyone we dealt with."

"Sounds like you were being groomed," Brianna commented.

Now wasn't the time to talk about family money, not when he could see that Brianna had clearly come up the hard way—and was still struggling.

Connor gave her his standard go-to reply. "Only to be good people and to work hard."

Again she caught herself envying him and the upbringing he'd had. The childhood he'd lived.

When his eyes met hers, she hid her feelings and smiled her approval. "Both very admirable qualities."

Chapter Eight

Connor had barely finished reading the notations in a quarter of the folders that Brianna had given him when his concentration was suddenly interrupted.

This time it wasn't because the sounds of a pint-size World War Three was breaking out somewhere in the house.

This particular interruption was an up close and personal one and came in the form of one Ava Susan Childress. That was how Brianna addressed her daughter in exasperation when the latter strode into her office and in a loud, intrusive voice asked her, "Are you finished with him yet?"

Startled—her children were supposed to be playing out in the yard—Brianna cried, "Ava Susan Childress, where are your manners? We don't ask questions like that," Brianna insisted.

Undaunted, her daughter actually looked rather upset over being unceremoniously called out on the carpet and admonished in this fashion. Cocking her small, silky dark brown head, she focused her bright blue eyes accusingly at her mother.

"Well, I did. I wanted to know if you were finished with him so he could tell us another story. It was for Axel, too," the little girl added, as if that should make everything all right. "He wanted to hear another story, too."

Brianna flashed an apologetic look toward the private investigator. As usual, her children had managed to embarrass her.

"I'm sorry about this," she told Connor.

Amused by the little girl's straightforward approach, he brushed off Brianna's apology.

"No need to be sorry," Connor assured her. The truth was, he was getting a kick out of all this. "I've never been in demand by members of the short person set before," he said with a grin.

Ava was trying hard to understand. "Does that mean he can go with me?" she wanted to know.

Axel appeared in the doorway. For once he was there to back up his sister instead of disputing every word she had to say.

"Mr. Fortunado doesn't take orders from me," Brianna informed her son and daughter. "He's here strictly as my client."

Connor saw the way the two children's faces fell. He looked from one to the other. They looked too young to know the meaning of the word *client*, so he asked Ava and Axel what they thought.

His eyes studied their expressions. "Do you know what the word *client* means?"

"Yeah," Ava answered. She slanted a grudging look toward her mother. "It means the person's important and we have to leave them alone." She ended with a rather dramatic sigh.

"Yeah, alone," Axel echoed, sticking out his lower lip and pouting.

"I see," Connor responded, looking at them thoughtfully. "Well, I'm not that kind of a client," he told them.

Hope instantly lit up the two small faces and they smiled.

"What kind of client are you?" Axel wanted to know.

"The kind that likes to take breaks so that he can tell two really great little people stories they want to hear," Connor answered, struggling not to laugh.

Ava's grin grew twice as large as it had when he'd first walked in today. "You mean like us?" she asked her new hero eagerly.

"Exactly like you," Connor replied.

Although it warmed Brianna's heart to see Connor being so nice to her children, it was a source of concern, as well. Ava and Axel had both taken to this man in an incredibly short amount of time, so short that it didn't even seem as if it was possible—except that they had.

Therein lay the problem. She didn't want her children getting used to having this man around because the moment he got all the information he was after, Connor would be gone, and Ava and Axel wouldn't be able to understand why he wasn't coming back anymore. They were sure to take it personally, she thought. They'd think it was because of something they had done.

She didn't want that happening.

It was one of the reasons she didn't date. The fact was, she wouldn't be dating for one, she'd actually be dating for three, and her children's feelings meant everything to her.

Looking at Connor over their heads now, Brianna's voice sounded a little strained as she told him, "You know you really don't have to do this."

He thought she was trying to ease him out of what she probably felt was an imposition by her children. He didn't see it as an imposition, though.

"That's okay, I don't mind," Connor told her. He was already trying to think of a story that he could tell the duo.

Ava and Axel somehow seemed to have surrounded him even though he was still just sitting at the desk. Their combined presence had a way of being overwhelming.

"No, *really*," Brianna emphasized, her eyes meeting his. "You don't have to do this."

Something in her tone caught Connor's attention and he tried to read between the lines, but failed. Transparency was *not* one of her strong suits, Connor thought.

So he decided to go the simple route and just ask her outright. "Are you saying that you *don't* want me to tell them a story?"

"Mama," Ava wailed in disappointment. She wanted to hear the story that Connor had to tell whatever it turned out to be.

Not to be left out, Axel joined in and cried in a loud voice, "Mom!"

With Connor clearly on their side, she knew she was outnumbered. Brianna retreated and surrendered. She was not about to be the bad guy today.

"Never mind," she told Connor, waving away the whole thing. "I just didn't want you to feel you were being guilted into anything."

He flashed another smile at Brianna as Axel climbed up onto one of his knees and Ava scaled the other. "Don't worry about me," he told their mother. "I can handle myself."

She highly doubted that, not when it came to her kids.

"Remember," she told him as she crossed the threshold out of her office, "you said it, I didn't."

Her departure took him by surprise. "You're leaving? Where are you going?" Connor wanted to know, calling after her. He had just assumed that Brianna would remain in the room along with her children.

"I've got a chicken to get into the oven," she tossed over her shoulder, never breaking stride.

Before he could say anything more, he felt two small hands on his face, turning it so that he found himself looking down into Ava's face rather than the doorway.

"Don't worry, the chicken's not alive," she assured him in a voice that very easily could have belonged to someone four times her age.

"Yeah, Mom gets them at the store and they're already dead," Axel said with authority, not to be left out of the conversation.

"Tell us about your horse," Ava prompted. "Did you put other clothes on him?"

Connor laughed. Obviously the story had left a big impression on the children. "No, my dad put an end to that pretty quick."

Ava was very quiet for a total of five seconds, and then she told him, "We don't have a dad. What's it like to have one?" she asked.

"Doesn't your dad let you play with your horse?" Axel wanted to know.

Connor thought about the annoyed look that had descended over Kenneth Fortunado's face when he told his father that he'd turned his back on the firm and decided to become a private investigator. That, he thought, had been the face of disapproval.

"Sometimes he can be difficult," Connor told his small audience, not really wanting to say anything derogatory about his father. He knew the man had been disappointed by the news, but in reality, it had been his decision to make.

Small, expressive eyebrows knitted themselves together over the bridge of Ava's nose. "What's diffy—diffy—that word you just said," Ava finally said, giving up.

"It means that sometimes my dad doesn't see things the way I do," Connor explained, wanting to leave it at that.

He hadn't reckoned on the inquisitive minds he was dealing with.

"Mama's like that all the time," Ava confided in a hushed voice that was a little louder than a stage whisper.

"Yeah," Axel cried, wiggling into the conversation, "she's always trying to get us not to do things because it makes her nervous."

"Well, being a mom for two smart kids can be pretty hard sometimes," Connor reminded them sympathetically. "I'm sure that your mother's just trying to do the best she can."

Ava apparently thought his words over before she nodded her head. "Yeah," Ava agreed. "She does. She doesn't even spank Axel when he's bad."

Rather than deny that he was bad, Axel just lumped her in with him. "You're bad, too," he insisted, looking pointedly at his sister. He was not about to take the blame alone.

The expression on Ava's face was indignant. "Am not!" she cried.

Axel did not go down without a fight. "Are, too!" he retorted.

Connor was beginning to catch on. This showed every sign of escalating. Connor quickly spoke up, raising his voice above theirs.

"Hey, hold it," he ordered. When they turned to look at him, he told them, "I don't think either one of you are bad."

Instead of their protesting his intrusion into their argument, Connor found himself looking down into two beaming faces.

"You don't?" the two cried in unison.

"No, I don't," he replied calmly.

The best way to handle the escalating feelings was to divert attention away from the cause. So he did.

"You want to talk about *bad*, you should have met

my brother Gavin when he was a kid. Now there was *bad*," he told them with feeling, although there was no judgment attached to the words. "My mom called it being mischievous." He laughed to himself. "But my dad just called it bad."

"Did Gavin get a lot of time-outs?" Axel wanted to know, no doubt thinking of the way he and his sister were punished.

"Time-outs?" Connor repeated. He decided to play along. The kids didn't need to hear every single fact that had been involved in Gavin and his upbringing. "Yeah, he got those, along with other things when he was particularly bad."

Axel rose to his knees, balancing himself on Connor's knee as he looked into his face. Small blue eyes probed his.

"What kind of things?" he wanted to know.

The boy made Connor think of someone who was afraid of horror movies but still wanted to go on watching to see what happened next.

"You don't want to talk about that," Connor told him casually. "Don't you want to hear about Manchester?"

Ava scrunched up her pretty little face, trying to understand. Axel appeared to be totally lost.

"What's a Man-chest-ta?" Ava asked.

Connor struggled to keep a straight face. "Manchester was my dog when I was growing up."

"You mean like Scruffy?" Ava asked eagerly. Like her mother, the little girl had an instant affinity for anything on four legs.

Connor glanced down at the dog that was never far away from at least one of the children if not both. A mixed breed, Scruffy looked as if he was part Chihuahua, part teacup poodle, with a little of something else thrown in.

The dog barely came up to the bottom of his shin. "Oh, a lot bigger than Scruffy," Connor told them. "Manchester was a Great Dane."

"What made him great?" Axel wanted to know, asking the question in all seriousness. "Was it something he did?"

It was harder and harder for Connor to continue maintaining a straight face. Instead of correcting the boy and possibly hurting his feelings, Connor told Axel in all solemnity, "He always came when I called."

"He doesn't do that anymore?" Ava asked, looking at her hero with sympathy.

Connor smiled at her, although the smile was a little sad around the edges. Manchester had always been his favorite dog. He had been almost inconsolable when the dog died. That had been years ago.

"I'm afraid he doesn't do anything anymore."

"Why?" Ava wanted to know.

Axel answered the question for her. "Because he's dead, stupid." He turned to look at Connor. "That's what you're trying to say, right?"

"Not in those words, no," Connor answered the little boy, then gently said, "And it's not nice to call your sister stupid."

Axel couldn't see why that was a problem. "But she is," he insisted.

"No, she isn't," Connor said kindly but firmly, "and you didn't mean that, either, did you?" he asked the boy. He smiled at the duo. "Someday you two are going to realize that you need to have each other's backs."

"Why?" Ava wanted to know, looking disdainfully at her brother. "I don't want his old back."

Again Connor had to struggle not to laugh. "Maybe not today, but you will soon," he said confidently. "That's what family does," he explained simply. "They take care of each other's backs."

From the look on her face, it still made no sense to Ava, although since Connor was her new hero, she seemed more than willing to be convinced.

"Do you have Gavin's back?" she wanted to know.

He smiled at the display of curiosity. "Yes, I do."

It was Axel's turn to ask a question. "Does he have yours?"

Turning to the boy, Connor nodded and said seriously, "He does."

Axel looked at his sister. It was obvious that he wasn't happy with this latest piece of information. "Do we have to?" he wanted to know, pained.

"You'll want to," Connor assured him. When he saw the dubious look crossing the little boy's face, he told him, "Trust me, you will."

Axel frowned but it was obvious he didn't want to oppose this new friend.

"If you say so," the little boy responded rather reluctantly.

Brianna stuck her head into the room. Part of her was surprised that Connor hadn't decided to bolt out of the house by now. The man had an amazing amount of patience and an incredible amount of staying power, she thought with admiration.

"You're still alive," she quipped, taking a step into the room.

He turned slightly to look at her. Perforce her children did, too. "You didn't expect me to be?" he asked, amused.

"Actually, at this point I expected you to be running for your life." With a smile, she nodded toward her children. "These two have been known to wear down concrete, and besides, this wasn't what you signed on for. Not in any manner," she added.

"Where did he sign, Mama?" Ava wanted to know. She wanted to know everything about this person her mother was working with.

"And what was it?" Axel asked in a louder voice, not to be outdone.

"Never mind, you two. Why don't you go outside again and play?" she suggested. "You've worn Mr. Fortunado down enough for one day."

"No, we didn't," Axel protested. "We didn't wear you down, did we?" he asked Connor, obviously regarding the man as a higher court of appeal.

Connor grinned, tickled at how seriously the boy viewed what his mother had said. "You didn't even scratch the surface," he replied.

"See?" Axel declared, looking at his mother. "We didn't even scratch anything."

Brianna felt drained. She decided to change the subject. She could tell that there was no winning this one.

"Dinner'll be ready in about forty-five minutes," she told the children. Then, looking at Connor, she added, "You're welcome to stay if you like."

"Yay!" Ava cried, clapping her hands. "Stay!"

"Yeah, stay!" Axel told him, adding his voice to his sister's.

It was hard to say no after that.

Connor turned his attention toward the woman who was sharing her research results with him. "Are you sure I won't be putting you out?"

"I wouldn't have extended the invitation if you were," she answered.

"Then I guess I'm staying," he said with a boyish grin.

Both children cheered again.

Chapter Nine

A schedule of sorts slowly emerged. Over the course of the next few days, Connor came over to her house and met with Brianna a number of times.

Admittedly, the young mother of two had given him enough information to set him on the right path. He had names and locations, not Charlotte's, but he felt that eventually, that would materialize. However, Connor still kept coming back to see her on the outside chance that there was perhaps even more that she could help him uncover.

Part of him secretly knew that what he was really doing was just coming up with excuses, giving himself reasons to continue seeing Brianna for just a little longer.

There was no question in his mind that he was attracted to her. Brianna had a rather memorable figure, even though all he had ever seen her wearing was jeans and a T-shirt. It really got to him. The amazing thing was that the woman didn't use any makeup or glamorous clothing to make herself look beautiful. Nevertheless, she just was.

Brianna was very simply a natural beauty, he thought. A natural beauty who would most likely turn him down if he asked her out, for the same reason she'd told him that they would have to work in her house—because of the children. She'd made it quite clear without actually stating it that Axel and Ava always came first.

The funny thing about it, Connor mused, here he was, a confirmed bachelor and he actually really *liked* her kids. In all honesty, he had never given much thought to kids at all, other than not wanting any. And yet, he liked hers.

Not because they were hers—if anything her children served as a reminder of the life Brianna had had with another man—but because both of them were so lively, so precocious and really amusing, the latter rather unwittingly.

"She's just the flavor of the month, that's all," he told himself. "Don't try to read anything more into it, Fortunado."

But even as he voiced what was his prevailing sentiment out loud in his car while he was driving to Brianna's house, Connor wasn't quite convincing himself that he was telling the truth.

That was because he found himself looking forward to seeing her—and those kids of hers—the way he couldn't remember looking forward to seeing *any* of the myriad of women who had passed through his life since just after his adolescence took hold.

"What the hell are you thinking?" he asked himself, annoyed. "You haven't even kissed the woman yet."

He wasn't attracted to her, Connor silently argued, he had just gotten caught up in a fantasy, that's all. All this wedding talk and planning had made him wonder what it would be like if he gave in to his family's pressure and joined the ranks of the newly married.

C'mon, Connor, get a grip. You don't want any of this. You're just curious, that's all.

He pushed all thoughts of Brianna and her children aside. Today would probably be the last time that he would be seeing any of them.

Or at least the second to last time, he amended— just in case.

Before he knew it, Connor found himself pulling up to the curb in front of Brianna's house.

How had that happened?

He had blanked out the entire way from his parents' estate to here, Connor realized. He supposed he should just be grateful that he hadn't gotten into some sort of an accident.

It was a sobering thought.

"He's here, Mama. He's here!" Ava announced excitedly, jumping up and down at the window in the living room.

Brianna automatically glanced at her watch, although there was really no need. The man had been turning up like clockwork every day.

"I'm going to let him in!" Ava declared, hurrying

from the window that faced the front of the house and running to the door.

"No, I am!" Axel announced, trying to beat his sister to the door.

"Neither one of you are opening the door," Brianna informed her children sternly. Short of putting a leash on them, how did she get this across to them? "Nothing's changed. You're still too young to open the door to anyone."

"But, Mama, it's Connor," Ava wailed, stopping— unwillingly—just short of the front door.

"It's who?" Brianna asked, looking pointedly at her daughter.

Ava sighed. It was a huge sigh for such a little girl. "Mr. Fortuna-dough," she dutifully said, correcting herself because that was what her mother was expecting to hear.

Brianna nodded. "Better."

Her eyes swept over the pint-size welcoming committee. Then, motioning both of her children aside, Brianna opened the door just as Connor was about to ring the bell.

He looked a little taken aback as he dropped his hand to his side again, then raised one quizzical eyebrow as his eyes met hers.

"My lookout told me you were coming up the front walk," Brianna explained.

"I was looking for you," Ava told him proudly, flashing a big grin.

"I was looking for you, too," Axel announced, not wanting to get lost in the shuffle. It was clear that because of his mother and his sister, he felt really out-numbered.

Before Connor could respond, Axel's eyes alighted on the big, flat box he was carrying. The boy's blue eyes all but shone with interest.

"Is that pizza?" Axel cried, not giving Connor a chance to comment on his sister's statement.

Rather than answer either of the children, Connor looked at their mother.

"I thought that I'd bring lunch with me and give you a break for a change." When she didn't say anything, he asked, "Is it okay?"

"It's a little late to ask that question, isn't it?" Brianna asked, amused that he'd think to ask her now. There was a lot to like about the man, Brianna thought.

Connor couldn't tell if he'd somehow offended her with this gesture, or if she really didn't mind. "We don't have to eat it," he told Brianna.

Axel looked as if he was about to burst into tears. "'Course we gotta eat it," he declared. "What else can you do with pizza?"

Ava took their cause to the highest authority—their mother. She looked at Brianna hopefully. "We can eat it, right, Mama?" she asked.

"Yes, you can eat it," Brianna agreed. "At lunch-time," she specified.

The last few days Connor had begun arriving at ten rather than after one, so she supposed it was only natural that one of these times he decided to bring a take-out lunch with him.

This time it was Axel who sighed mightily. "Okay,"

he agreed with something less than wholehearted enthusiasm.

"Yes, Mama," Ava's voice mimicked her brother's submissive tone.

"And only after you both say 'thank you' to Mr. Fortunado," she told them.

Both children turned toward the newcomer in their lives.

"Thank you!" Ava and Axel cried almost in unison. This time there was no mistaking the enthusiasm in their voices.

"My pleasure," Connor told the duo, pretending to bow his head in acknowledgment to their thanks.

"Now go clean up your room," Brianna told them. "Mr. Fortunado and I have work to do." The long faces were not lost on Brianna. "It's either that, or you go out and play in the backyard."

That required no prolonged debate at all. Axel made his choice instantly. "Play!"

"We'll go play," Ava told her mother with no hesitation.

Brianna waited until her children had dashed out of the room and gone out to play before she turned toward Connor holding the pizza box. She wasn't sure if he was just being generous, or if he felt that she was having trouble feeding him as well as her children.

"You didn't have to bring lunch," she told him.

"You fed me. I thought it was only fair that I return the favor, at least once." Connor realized it was a slip of the tongue the second he'd said it. He hadn't meant to say "at least once." That meant he had plans to come back for lunch again—and he didn't. He didn't want it

Dear Reader,

IT'S A FACT: if you answer 4 quick questions, we'll send you **4 FREE REWARDS!**

I'm not kidding you. As a leading publisher of women's fiction, we value your opinions… and your time. That's why we are prepared to **reward** you handsomely for completing our mini-survey. In fact, we have 4 Free Rewards for you, including 2 free books and 2 free gifts.

As you may have guessed, that's why our mini-survey is called **"4 for 4".** Answer 4 questions and get 4 Free Rewards. It's that simple!

Thank you for participating in our survey,

Pam Powers

To get your 4 FREE REWARDS:
Complete the survey below and return the insert today to receive 2 FREE BOOKS and 2 FREE GIFTS guaranteed!

"4 for 4" MINI-SURVEY

1 Is reading one of your favorite hobbies?
☐ YES   ☐ NO

2 Do you prefer to read instead of watch TV?
☐ YES   ☐ NO

3 Do you read newspapers and magazines?
☐ YES   ☐ NO

4 Do you enjoy trying new book series with FREE BOOKS?
☐ YES   ☐ NO

YES! I have completed the above Mini-Survey. Please send me my 4 FREE REWARDS (worth over $20 retail). I understand that I am under no obligation to buy anything, as explained on the back of this card.

235/235 HDL GNRV

FIRST NAME	LAST NAME

ADDRESS

APT.#	CITY

STATE/PROV.	ZIP/POSTAL CODE

to sound as if he was committing to anything—because he wasn't, he silently insisted.

"Well, I appreciate it," she told him crisply, trying her best to be gracious.

Brianna took the pizza into the kitchen. When he followed her, she took advantage of having him there. Still holding the box, she turned toward him.

"Would you mind putting it on that shelf?" she asked, pointing to the highest shelf in the pantry.

He looked a little bemused. "Why not just leave it on the counter?"

"Simple. I don't want Ava and Axel succumbing to temptation," she told him. Passing the box to him, Brianna caught a whiff of the pizza. "That does smell good," she commented with appreciation.

What he caught a whiff of was not the pizza but the very light fragrance that Brianna tended to wear. Something delicate and flowery. It made him think of that old line about stopping to smell the roses.

"Yes, it does," he agreed in a low, appreciative voice.

Brianna felt a wave of heat flash over her entire body.

If she didn't know better, she would have said that Connor wasn't really talking about the pizza.

But of course he had to be, she told herself the next moment. She was letting her imagination get the better of her.

"Um, you can put the box right up there," she told him, pointing up to the shelf above her.

As Connor started to do as she instructed, the corner of the pizza box accidentally hit a box of rice that was precariously perched on the edge of that shelf, knocking it down. The box of rice flipped as it fell and since it apparently had been opened, it rained grains of rice all over Brianna.

More than a little of the rice wound up in her hair.

Connor really didn't want to laugh. He had a feeling that it would either make Brianna angry or embarrass her. But he couldn't help himself. She did look rather adorable with all that rice looking as if it was woven through her hair.

"I am sorry," he apologized, losing his struggle not to laugh as he quickly brushed as much rice out of her hair as he could.

"That would sound a little more believable if you weren't laughing," she told him.

He noted with relief that Brianna didn't seem to be angry.

"Sorry," Connor apologized again, biting his lip to keep a laugh back. "I'm not laughing," he protested, although not very believably.

"Your eyes are laughing," Brianna pointed out.

"No, they're not," he protested.

Connor continued brushing the rice out of her hair, doing his best to focus on getting the grains out and not looking at her.

"I'm not very good at this," he confessed ruefully. He reached around her to get the rice at the back of her head.

Somehow, as he did so, Connor wound up getting much too close to her. That, in turn, led to something else. Something he hadn't counted on.

Before Connor could stop himself, he kissed her.

It was hard to say who that surprised more, him or her.

Connor fully expected her to pull away. But she didn't.

And he couldn't.

At that moment it occurred to him that he had been wondering all along what it would feel like to kiss Brianna. To press his lips against hers with feeling.

When it happened, he couldn't really begin to describe it. Couldn't encapsulate the sensation into words.

He just went with it, losing himself in the taste of her lips and reveling in it.

Just like that, Brianna lost all concept of time and place, feeling as if she'd suddenly fallen through the mythical rabbit hole and rather than try to pull herself out of it, she just continued to free-fall, to whirl around within the endless, bottomless cylinder.

All she could do was to draw in the delicious sensation vibrating through her and—just for the moment— allow herself to enjoy it.

Pleasure reached out to every single part of her.

What if the kids come in now?

The sudden thought flashed through her mind and was enough to startle her back to reality. Brianna pulled her head away from him.

She was breathing very hard. It took a great deal of concentration to get herself under control and not sound as if she'd just raced up three flights of stairs doing double time.

Connor looked at her as if he had never seen her before and maybe he hadn't.

Not in this light.

By doing nothing else except kissing him back, Brianna had knocked his proverbial socks off.

He had not seen that coming, and at first, he didn't know how to handle it—or himself.

"Sorry," he mumbled.

Brianna thought he was apologizing for kissing her and she didn't want him to.

"For knocking over the box and getting all that rice in your hair," he said, completing the sentence.

He *wasn't* apologizing for kissing her, she thought. She hadn't expected to be so happy and relieved that he wasn't.

Despite having a relationship in her past and two children from that relationship, this was all brand-new to her.

"That's all right," she finally replied. "I don't remember when I put that rice up there. It was probably stale anyway, being opened like that for who knows how long."

Connor looked around at the mess that had spilled out all over the floor. "You have a broom around somewhere?" he wanted to know. "I'll clean all this up."

The offer caught her off guard even more than the falling box of rice had. In all their time together, Jonny had never lifted a finger to help her around the house. He'd get up from the table leaving his dishes, and any clothes he took off wound up on the floor. It got to the point where she just accepted that as normal male behavior. Obviously, it wasn't.

"You're serious?" she asked Connor.

"I knocked it over. I should be the one who cleans it up," he told her.

"Okay." Brianna opened the door to the tall, narrow closet located opposite the pantry. Taking out the broom and dustpan, she held out both to Connor. "Take your pick," she said. When he reached for the broom, she said, "Okay, I'll hold the dustpan."

"Teamwork," he said with an approving smile. "And by the way, I'll pay for the rice," he added as an afterthought.

"I already told you, it was probably stale at this point. Besides, that was the store's own brand," she told Connor. "It didn't exactly cost me a king's ransom." She squatted down, holding the dustpan in position as he swept up the rice.

It wasn't just the cost, it was the inconvenience—and his being clumsy, Connor thought. "I still feel bad about knocking it over."

Brianna waved away his guilt as she rose to her feet and dumped the rice into the garbage. Turning, she squatted down again, holding the dustpan in place for Connor.

"You bought lunch, I absolve you. Consider us even," she said.

"Speaking of even," he said, getting the last of the rice. "Have you deposited the check yet?"

Brianna emptied the dustpan, then placed it back in the closet. She was stalling, trying to brace herself for what possibly might be coming. Was he going to tell her that he'd changed his mind about paying her? Or was he going to say that there were no funds to cover the check after all?

"I was going to do that Friday," she said. "Do you want me to hold off?"

He looked surprised that she would ask that. "No, I was just wondering why the check hadn't been accounted for yet."

Her smile was somewhat sheepish as she admitted, "I just wanted to hold on to it in case you decided that you changed your mind."

He handed her back the broom. "Cash it," he instructed. "The funds aren't going anywhere."

And neither was he, he silently added.

For now.

Chapter Ten

He caught himself watching Brianna while they all ate lunch.

Watching her and thinking.

It surprised Connor that he had mixed feelings about what had just happened between them. Normally, whenever he kissed a woman, no matter who initiated the kiss, it registered as a pleasurable experience, one that, on most occasions, led to something more physical. But then, for one reason or another, the effects would always fade and he would move on to something else.

To some*one* else.

But this time it was different. Or it *would* be different, he thought. If he was inclined to get involved with Brianna. What made it different was that she came as a package deal. There were children to consider. Children he actually found himself liking.

Children who would be hurt once he left, he thought. Because he *always* left. No matter how long or short the relationship lasted, he never committed to to it, not in any sort of a permanent way. It just wasn't him.

And yet…

There was no "yet," he silently insisted. Whatever this strange feeling was, it would be over with soon enough. And he'd be home again, living the high life again.

He couldn't think about this now, Connor silently insisted. He had a dangerous woman to track down and catch and everything else had to come second—if it came at all. Which it wouldn't, he promised himself. Right now, he still had credit card activity to follow up on. The woman had to be out there somewhere.

A small, high-pitched voice broke into his thoughts, scattering them.

"Why aren't you talking?" Ava wanted to know, looking up at Connor.

To cover his temporary lapse, Connor said the first thing that came to his mind. "Because I'm busy eating."

"I can eat and talk at the same time," Axel told him. "Why can't you?"

This time it was Brianna who came to his rescue. "Because it's not polite to talk with your mouth full," she told her son.

"I don't," Axel protested, looking hurt as he looked at his mother. "I chew fast. See?" he asked, giving her a demonstration that involved chewing and then opening his mouth for his mother.

"Oooh, gross!" Ava cried, wrinkling her nose.

"Make him close his mouth!" Her request was directed toward Connor. "He'll listen to you."

This was getting out of hand, Brianna thought. First he'd thrown her for a loop by kissing her, and now her children were acting out because of him.

"Axel, behave," Brianna ordered. "You, too, Ava," she told her daughter, who had started to laugh at her brother, pointing a finger at him because he'd been called out.

"What did I do?" Ava wanted to know, pouting.

"Axel, Ava, Mr. Fortunado was nice enough to bring over pizza for the two of you. At least try to behave like little people instead of little wild animals," Brianna requested.

Grateful to have something to focus on besides his confused feelings toward Brianna, Connor looked at her two children.

"Would you two have liked me to bring something else for lunch besides pizza?" he asked.

"Oh no, we love pizza," Axel told him with feeling, stressing the word *love*.

"We'd eat it every day if Mama let us," Ava said, bobbing her head.

"But then it wouldn't be special, would it?" Connor pointed out.

"Yes it would," Axel said with conviction. "There're so many different kinds of pizza to eat," the little boy told him.

"Well, that answer's too smart for me," Connor told Axel, pretending to surrender. He glanced at Brianna. "You've got a couple of special kids here," he told her.

Axel and Ava were both beaming at the compliment.

Brianna loved seeing them like that—proud and *quiet*, she thought, suppressing a grin. She raised her eyes to Connor's. Just for a moment, she wondered what it would have been like if *he* had been their father instead of Jonny, wherever he was now.

That thought pulled her up short. She couldn't let herself go there. There was no point in fantasizing about something that didn't even have a prayer of happening. She had too much to deal with right now to let her mind wander like that.

"I guess I do at that," she agreed quietly.

The pizza disappeared in an amazingly short amount of time.

Moving slightly back from the table, Connor held his stomach as if it ached. "I think I ate too much," he groaned.

"*You* ate too much?" Brianna laughed. Despite cautioning them, Axel and Ava had wolfed down their food as if it was the last they would see for a long time. "These two ate so much I'm surprised they're not exploding."

Axel's eyes widened in fear. "Can we do that?" he asked not his mother but Connor, who seemed to be his go-to authority on everything. "Can we explode?"

Connor tried to recall if he had ever been this literal when he'd been Axel's age, but he couldn't remember. Whether or not he was, he was quick to set the boy's mind at ease without directly contradicting his mother.

"You have a long, long way to go before that ever happens," he assured Axel and his sister. "But all that food might have made you sleepy. You might want to take a nap."

"No, no naps," Axel cried with a little less vigor than he would have been inclined to display if he'd been less full.

"How about playing a quiet game, then?" Connor suggested, thinking that doing anything more strenuous right now might cause the boy to throw up.

Axel's eyes lit up. "Sure! What kind of a game you wanna play?"

"I wanna play, too!" Ava said eagerly, adding her voice to that of her brother. She made it clear that she wasn't going to be left out.

"I didn't—"

How had this happened? Connor wondered, stunned. He hadn't meant that he wanted to play a game with them, only that they should play a game with each other. He was just trying to come up with something they could do that didn't require them being physically taxed.

Brianna felt sorry for him. She knew exactly what it was like to feel outnumbered by the twosome. "I think that Mr. Fortunado meant that you two should be the ones to find a game to play," she told her children as she stacked all their dishes together.

"No, he didn't," Axel protested fiercely. And then the little boy turned to look at Connor, expecting the man to back him up. "Did you?"

Connor had never had trouble saying no to people, not even to his superiors if he felt strongly about something. He'd always been the kind of person who stuck to his guns no matter what the situation was. But to his dismay, he found that when two small, sad faces looked up at him hopefully, the word *no* was somehow emulsified, vanishing from the face of the earth.

"You're right," he told them, nodding his head. "I didn't."

Oh Lord, she didn't want to lose her heart to this man, she really didn't. It was only asking for trouble, she thought. She'd been that route and wound up having her heart handed back to her, crushed and carelessly stuffed into a plastic bag like so much confetti.

But reason just wasn't working here. She could feel her heart slipping away from her and moving toward this man who had fixed her toilet rather than tell her that she'd made a mistake. This man who gave in to her children rather than disappoint them by just shrugging them off and turning away.

Each of the children grabbed one of his hands, pulling him to his feet. "Looks like they have plans for me," Connor said as they began to drag him away.

Brianna rose, holding the stacked dishes. "Do you want to be rescued?" she asked him, ready to call off her children if he gave the word.

His grin was amused rather than martyr-like. "Not particularly."

"Okay," she said, backing off. "Just remember," she told him, smiling despite her attempts to keep a straight face, "this was your idea." She'd been saying that to him a lot lately.

"C'mon," Axel cried, tugging insistently on his hand. "No more talking to Mom. The game's in our room."

She saw Connor looking over his shoulder at her. He actually looked as if he was enjoying himself, she thought. "I'll be in their room."

"I know where that is," Brianna replied, humoring him. "I'll be working in my office," she wanted him to know. She said the words just before he disappeared around the corner.

Brianna turned to go back to her office. She could hear Ava's and Axel's gleeful laughter floating down the hall from the opposite direction.

It's just a game he's going to be playing with them. Don't overthink this and don't get carried away, she warned herself.

But it was really hard not to.

By the time Connor finally walked into her office, it was more than two hours later.

She was aware of his presence before she even turned around. Somehow, the very air felt different to her.

"I was getting ready to send out a search party for you," Brianna quipped.

He laughed, not at her but at his own part in this. "Every time I started to get up after a game was over, they talked me into playing 'just one more,'" he told her, sitting down in the extra chair she'd brought into the room. The chair had eaten up what little space was left within the office.

"Your kids can be very persuasive," Connor informed her.

Brianna laughed. "You realize that you're preaching to the choir," she told him. "It turns out that everything with them is always a negotiation, or a battle of wills. You'd think that kids so young would go along with everything I tell them to do. Ha!"

She laughed at the very notion of complete, uncomplicated obedience from her children. That would be the day, she thought. And, although it might be nice once in a while, she really did love their spirit. Just as she loved them.

"Half the time you'd think that they were the parents and I was the kid."

In his opinion, Brianna sounded as if she was being too hard on herself. "Oh, I don't know. I think you've done a pretty good job raising them."

"All smoke and mirrors," she confessed. "I'm really just hanging on by my fingertips."

"And you've raised them without any help?" he asked. She'd told him that the children's father had walked out on her, but maybe there was someone else she could turn to, someone to help her, like a relative who was there for her.

But the next moment, she shook her head, letting him know that she hadn't done absolutely *everything* by herself.

"Occasionally, I get a sitter to stay with them and there's Beth Wilson." She saw curiosity enter Connor's eyes.

"She's the mother of two kids who are about Ava and Axel's age. She watches them when I go in to my two other jobs, but I'm not at either one of those places for long periods of time," she said quickly.

"So what you're saying is that there's really no one

you can turn to for help with the kids on a long-term basis," Connor concluded.

"No, not on a long-term basis," Brianna confirmed. With a sigh she told him, "For better or worse, it's mostly me."

"Oh, I think it's for the better," Connor said with feeling. "Definitely for the better."

Brianna turned all the way around from her desk and looked at him, confused.

"I don't know why you're being so nice to me. My kids must have run you ragged these last two hours. I know what they're like when they get someone to play a game with them. I know they appreciate it, but actual war games are a lot easier to handle than playing with those two."

He laughed, amused by the comparison. "Oh, it wasn't so bad. I had fun."

The man obviously had a strange definition of *fun*, Brianna thought.

"Now you're just lying," she told him.

"No, I'm not," he assured Brianna. "Ava and Axel can be very entertaining when they want to."

She knew that she felt that way, but she had an excuse. She was their mother. Connor was someone who had absolutely no ties to her children, nothing to be gained by going easy on them or professing that he was enjoying himself.

Brianna looked at him closely, scrutinizing the man. He didn't look any different than he had before, but it really wasn't adding up.

"What did my kids do to you?" she wanted to know.

He laughed. Another woman would have taken the

easy way out and not pressed. She obviously valued honesty more.

"Nothing. They just reminded me what it was like to be their age. It's been a long time since I had such an innocent view of the world."

"Do you have any kids?" she asked, realizing that she knew nothing about this man who had invaded her children's lives and her own.

"Kids?" he repeated. "Oh God, no. They wouldn't fit into the life I have in Denver."

Denver. The man lived in Denver. And he made it sound as if he didn't want kids. Brianna felt her heart drop. Boy, she could sure pick 'em, she thought ruefully.

"Yes, well, listen," she said, rallying, "if they wore you out and you want to call it a day, I totally understand. You can come back tomorrow and we'll pick up where we left off. I'll be here—at least, in the morning," she clarified.

"Oh? Where'll you be in the afternoon?" he asked her before he thought better of it. It wasn't any of his business, he thought.

But he still wanted to know.

"I promised to fill in at the reception desk. Emily, the woman who's usually there tomorrow, has to take the afternoon off," she explained, "so they need me to come in. Unfortunately Beth isn't available so…"

"You need someone to watch the kids?"

Her kids were far too young to be left alone. Finding someone to watch them was on her to-do list today.

"Well, it's either that or not come home to a house," she told him simply.

He saw the wary look in her eyes. He didn't want to put her off. He needed her help. Connor realized that he needed to make amends, even if this wasn't his forte. "Why don't I watch the kids for you?" Connor volunteered. "That way, you won't have to pay a sitter and the kids already know me." He smiled at her. "They won't have to get used to anyone new."

Brianna looked at him, totally taken aback. "You really are a glutton for punishment, aren't you?" she marveled.

"No, I really enjoy it," he insisted. He was lying, but she didn't need to know that, he thought. He looked down and saw that Juliana, the calico cat who was the latest addition to Brianna's menagerie, was batting his pant cuff back and forth. Connor's eyes crinkled. "All of it," he added, amused. His words surprised him more than they did her.

"You say that now. Wait until Juliana misses and winds up scratching up your leg," Brianna predicted ominously.

Bending over, Brianna picked up the cat and carried her out of the room. She put the animal down and then retreated back into her office, this time closing the door behind her to keep the cat out.

"You're closing the door," Connor pointed out. Was that on purpose or by mistake? "Does that mean you want me to stay?"

Oh Lord, yes, Brianna thought, suddenly remembering the way his lips had felt against hers.

Because she found herself longing to feel that sensation again and knew how dangerous that was for her in her present state of mind, especially given that there was no future for them, Brianna said the first thing that came to mind.

"Actually, I didn't mean to close the door. It's just to discourage the cat. Just give it five minutes and then you can go. Otherwise, she might still be hanging around. Once she sees you again, she'll just exert her little feline wiles on you. Before you know it, you'll find Juliana wrapped around your leg or some other vital part you can't do without."

He laughed. "Everything about you is intriguing, Brianna. Even your pets."

"They all have unique personalities if that's what you mean. Actually, they're all strays. Or they were before I took them in." Brianna smiled ruefully.

She knew how that had to sound to someone who wasn't moved by stray animals.

"I have a penchant for attracting strays and trying to fix them," she admitted.

It had been that way all of her life, she thought. Jonny had just been another lost stray who she had tried to fix—and failed.

He had a feeling he knew where she was going with this. "I'm not a stray, Brianna," he assured her.

She looked away, pretending to look for something on her desk. "I didn't say you were."

He ignored her protest. Neither one of them believed it. "And you won't have to fix me."

She smiled then. Her eyes met his. "That's a matter of opinion."

Intrigued, he asked, "You think I need fixing?"

"I think everyone needs fixing to some extent," she said evasively. "Some more than others."

"Interesting idea," he told her. "Maybe we'll pick this up when I come back tomorrow."

Brianna merely smiled. "You're the client."

Right. Then why did he feel like she was the one in the driver's seat?

Chapter Eleven

When he came over to Brianna's house the following day, Connor went through what had by now become his usual ritual: greeting Axel and Ava and answering any of their questions.

It amazed him how two young children could come up with so many different questions to ask each and every time.

Eventually, Brianna managed to herd the two away, directing her children either to the yard, the living room or their room, and they were always prevailed upon to go play, which they did, but never without protest.

"They certainly are a handful," Connor commented, not for the first time, as he followed her into her office. "Dealing with all this every day, how do you manage to stay sane?"

She grinned at him. "Who says I'm sane?"

"Well, you seem pretty sane to me," Connor told her.

"And the illusion continues," Brianna said cryptically.

Pausing at her desk, she picked up several folders she'd been working on and handed them to Connor. "These are all the rest of the names I managed to track down for Charlene—Charlotte." Brianna corrected herself before Connor could.

Connor accepted the folders from her, folders it was now obvious that she had placed elsewhere once the project had been suspended.

He knew that she had to have unearthed them after doing some really intensive searching through the plastic drawers she referred to as her "filing cabinet."

"What's that?" he asked, nodding at a stray paper on top. At first glance it looked like a photocopied list of names.

She didn't have to look to know what he was referring to. "Those are the names I didn't get a chance to look for," Brianna explained.

Connor wasn't sure if he understood her. "Come again?"

Taking the adjacent chair, she pulled it closer to the desk and sat down facing Connor. "Well, initially, this Charlotte person sent me about ten names, all people she wanted to locate. I reported back to her regularly on my progress and, like I said, she paid half up front and promised the rest when I finished. But she kept adding names to that list and there turned out to be a great many people who weren't exactly easy to find, so I concentrated on the ones that I *could* find and did those first.

"When she didn't make good on her payment for the

next installment of reports I sent her, I stopped trying to locate people. I was waiting for her to live up to her side of the deal," she confessed. Brianna shrugged, at a loss. "She never got back to me and then I got that Return to Sender letter back in the mail. Since she'd made it clear through her actions that she wasn't going to pay any more money and that she obviously didn't want to be found herself, I didn't continue looking for any of these other people."

"Wow," he murmured under his breath as he thumbed through the remaining list of names. "But you think you can find these people?" he asked.

"Well, I can't promise anything," Brianna told him cautiously, "but I can certainly try."

He looked at the list again. It astonished him how one man could have been responsible for bringing so many people into the world. Finding them was going to be a big job, he thought.

"I'll pay you, of course," he told Brianna in case he hadn't made that clear to her.

"In addition to the three thousand dollars you've already paid?" she asked him, surprised.

"Well, sure," he told her. He didn't expect her to do this strictly out of charity. This was going to take effort. "This is additional work on your part." He saw the puzzled expression on her face. "What?"

"I have to ask," Brianna told him, concerned that maybe she was getting involved in something that had more to it than there seemed to be on the surface. She knew she'd already asked him once before without really getting an answer, but this time she felt she needed it. She didn't want to risk getting involved in something illegal. "Why are you trying to find the same people that this woman was looking for?"

Connor debated whether or not to tell her. Quite honestly, he'd been feeling rather guilty about keeping Brianna in the dark this way—not that any of this would affect her. She certainly wasn't in any danger the way some, if not all, of the people on that list were. The list, if he were to take a guess, contained the names of all the family members who were related to Gerald Robinson either directly or indirectly.

And Charlotte, he knew, hated all of them. Not in principle, but in actual fact. In his estimation, the woman was a walking psycho. Gerald leaving Charlotte to be with his "first love" had obviously pushed the woman over the edge and now she was bent on getting her revenge on the whole lot of them.

Brianna was still looking at him, waiting for an answer.

Connor made up his mind.

"To warn them," he told her.

"Warn them?" she repeated, no less confused than she had been a moment ago. "Warn them about what?" she wanted to know.

That was just it. He didn't know any of the actual particulars. Didn't know what further mayhem Charlotte was capable of.

Frustrated, he told Brianna, "That they could be in danger."

She felt as if they were taking baby steps here, trying to get to the truth. "From what?"

"From Charlotte," he said bluntly.

Ordinarily, she'd just back away and let him keep

whatever secret he was trying to preserve. But she'd come this far, she wasn't about to stop until he gave her an answer that made some sense to her.

"I don't understand."

She was an outsider, not family, but in his opinion, Brianna had earned the right to know some things. "It's my feeling that Charlotte wants to hurt as many of these people as she can."

"But why?" Brianna pressed. Why would anyone want to hurt people she didn't even know or had never met?

"It's complicated," he told her, thinking of all the stories he'd come across regarding Gerald Robinson.

She knew what that meant, Brianna thought, frowning. "So you're not going to tell me," she guessed.

He blew out a breath. The die had been cast. "No, I am. You just have to keep a very open mind," he warned. When Brianna nodded, Connor began. "In a nutshell, some of the people on this list are her husband's offspring and she's determined to track them all down."

"His offspring?" Brianna repeated, stunned. "There's got to be almost twenty-five people on that list. Maybe even more."

She wasn't saying anything that he wasn't aware of. "I know."

"And you're telling me that they're all his—his children?" she asked incredulously, still unable to wrap her mind around what Connor was saying.

He laughed dryly. There was no humor in the sound. "The man got around. But this also includes his half brothers' kids."

Brianna's eyes widened as she looked at all the names on the list again. Names of people she'd searched for and found. Names of people she hadn't gotten around to looking for. And names of people she'd looked for but hadn't found. And all these people were most likely in the dark about their family tree.

It was beginning to make a little sense to her now. "Is that why you're trying to find them first?" she asked Connor. "So you can find a way to break it to them to minimize their getting hurt?"

Connor shook his head. "If that was the only thing, I'd just let it all go and hope for the best. It's really none of my business if they know or don't know. But I honestly don't know how far Charlotte will go in order to get her revenge." He frowned, thinking of the havoc the woman had already caused. "She's already done a lot of damage."

"What's she done?" Brianna wanted to know.

She looked so innocent, for a second, he had second thoughts about exposing her to all this ugliness. But he wanted her help, so he told her.

"For openers, I'm ninety-nine point nine percent positive that she's the one who burned down Gerald Robinson's mansion."

Stunned, Brianna asked, "She's an arsonist?"

Connor nodded. "That's what I think." Since he'd opened the door on this, he continued. "And she's also behind the creative sabotage that caused Fortunado Real Estate to lose so many clients, not to mention the cyberattack on Robinson Tech," he added grimly.

They were back to this not making any sense to her. "If this Charlotte woman is behind a cyberattack, what did she need me for?" Anyone capable of launching a cyberattack was able to find people using the internet.

He'd already thought about that. "I think she approached you first. The cyberattack happened just in the last couple of months." Charlotte was either upping her game, or finding people willing to do her bidding for a price without asking any questions.

"Maybe I should be happy that she disappeared out of my life." It was clear to Brianna that she had dodged a bullet.

He put his hand over hers. "Unless you have the bad luck of being one of Gerald's multitude of kids, I don't think you have anything to worry about."

A person who was so out for revenge didn't always stay within the lines, she knew. "But you can't be sure."

"You're right, I can't," Connor agreed. "But I'd say Charlotte's too focused on hurting her ex-husband's progeny to waste her time and effort on hurting an outsider."

Brianna shook her head, still having trouble taking all this in. She hadn't had an easy time of it in her life, but she couldn't visualize the kind of anger that would make someone plot this sort of far-reaching revenge. Or any kind of revenge for that matter.

"It's hard to believe that someone can be this eaten up by hate," she told him.

Connor smiled at her as he tucked a bit of stray hair behind Brianna's ear. "You really are a good person, Brianna," he commented.

She wasn't so sure about that. Good people didn't have these sorts of feelings rushing through them in response to someone just casually brushing against their skin.

"Not all the time," she finally told him quietly.

Damn it, they were sitting here talking about Charlotte, the Dragon Lady. The very personification of evil. So why, in the middle of all this, was he suddenly wanting Brianna? And why, in the middle of all this, of discovering that there were more people he had to find, to warn, was he suddenly consumed with the desire to possess this woman?

She was the single mother of two little kids, kids she was struggling every day to provide for. He had no right to disrupt her life because he wanted her.

No right at all.

It didn't seem to matter.

Logic was not getting in his way. It was *not* keeping him from leaning into her and rediscovering just how sweet her mouth was.

And it was.

It was very, very sweet, he thought, as what had begun as just a quick kiss flowered into something a great deal more. Something that shook him down to his very toes even as it begged him to go on, to lose himself in all that Brianna had to offer.

Oh Lord, she had promised herself that this wasn't going to happen again, that she wouldn't get close enough to him physically to be tempted to relive that spectacular kiss that she had sampled the other day. And yet, here she was again, feeling her heart slamming against her chest so hard, she thought her ribs would crack. This kiss was stealing away her very breath even as it somehow managed to magically dim the very sunlight that had, until a second ago, been in the room.

Struggling, she managed to gather what little strength she had left and somehow pulled her head back.

"I can't do this," she told him, trying very hard not to sound as if she was breathless. "I can't get involved with you." Her eyes pleaded with him to understand. "It's not that I don't want to, but I have to think of the kids."

"They like me," he reminded her, his voice surrounding her. Keeping her warm.

"That's just the problem. They *like* you," she told him. "They're used to you. And you're not going to be staying." She released a shaky breath, searching for words to make him understand why she was pushing him away. "You don't even live in Houston," she cried. "When we finish finding those people on that list—when we finish our business together—you'll be gone and…they'll be devastated."

She'd almost said that she would be devastated but stopped herself at the last moment. He didn't need to know that.

"I've got to remember that and not let them sense that there's anything going on between us," Brianna told him. "Because then they'd really think that you were going to stay."

"They won't know," he argued.

Connor realized that he was pleading his case without actually saying the words—but he *was* pleading. Because that was how much he wanted her.

She shook her head, dismissing his words. "They're kids. Kids intuit things. They'll know." She willed herself to fight back tears. "I'm sorry, Connor, but I can't."

"No, I'm the one who's sorry," he told her with emotion. "For a lot of reasons." Connor raised his hands like someone who was backing off from something he desperately wanted to touch. "Don't worry, I'll back off," he promised. "You don't have anything to worry about from me, Brianna. I give you my word. Scout's honor," he added with a wink.

She sincerely doubted that the man sitting at the desk right next to her had ever been a Boy Scout, but she pretended to take him at his word.

After all, it wasn't as if she had any other choice available to her.

Any further discussion of this truce they had awkwardly struck was suddenly tabled as it became clear to them that they were not alone. And this time, it wasn't one of the pets that had come wandering into the office.

Instead, it was Ava.

Brianna forced a smile to her face as she looked at her daughter. "What are you doing here, sugarplum? I thought you were playing with Axel."

"He's in the bathroom," Ava dutifully informed her mother with a shrug just before she dropped her bombshell. Turning toward Connor, she asked, "Were you kissing Mama?"

Connor was very grateful that he hadn't just taken a sip of the coffee he had brought into the room earlier. If he had, right now he'd either be choking or spraying it all over everything like a human geyser.

It took a minute for him to clear his throat sufficiently to speak.

"I'm sorry, what?" he asked. He was trying to stall

as his mind raced around for the right way to answer
Ava's question without either feeding her young imagination or lying.

"Were you kissing Mama?" she repeated, then told
him guilelessly, "It looked like you were."

"How do you know about kissing?" Brianna asked
her younger child.

Ava gave her mother a look that all but said: You
have to be kidding. She tossed her head. "I know about
kissing, Mama."

"Your mother had something in her eye," Connor
spoke up out of the blue. "I had to get in close so I
could get it out."

"Oh." The answer seemed to satisfy the little girl.
She bobbed her head up and down. "Okay." And then
she looked at Connor intently. "Are you finished in
here with Mama yet?"

"No, not yet," Connor answered, hoping she was
asking if he was finished working and not if he was
finished kissing her mother.

Again Ava nodded. "Okay. Come find me when you
are," she told him just before she made her way out of
the room again. A small adult trapped in a child's body.

Brianna turned to look at him. There was no need
for words. The expression on her face said it all. That
what had just happened proved her point and backed
up the reasons why she couldn't afford to get involved
with him no matter how tempting that was.

He took his cue and got as comfortable as he could
sitting at her desk. "I guess we'd better get back to
work before Ava comes looking for me again."

She'd never seen her daughter like this, or her son

for that matter. Both of her children had taken to Connor almost instantly. She'd be more than happy about that if she and Connor were serious about one another.

But no matter what she might feel, she could tell that Connor was not the type to get serious about anyone, not in the true sense of the word. Not when *serious* meant everlasting commitment. Connor represented the exact opposite of that. He was the very definition of a carefree bachelor and she was certain that he intended to stay that way.

And as long as he felt that way, she was not about to let her guard down and let him in.

She couldn't.

Chapter Twelve

Right after he fulfilled his babysitting obligation, he tried to stay away, he really did.

Full of selfless, altruistic intentions, Connor's resolution to keep his distance from Brianna lasted all of one day before finally crumbling.

The so-called leads that he told himself he needed to run down turned out to be nothing more than paper trails that really led nowhere.

Just as he suspected they would.

Presently, the most useful information he had to work with was all coming out of Brianna's past efforts on behalf of Charlotte, as well as the efforts she was putting into working with the list of names that Charlotte had forwarded to her.

So, after spending what felt like a completely restless night tossing and turning in his bed and then coming up with every excuse he could think of not to turn up on her doorstep, Connor turned up on Brianna's doorstep the following afternoon.

Even so, standing before her door, he wrestled with his conscience, raising his hand and then dropping it to his side before he could ring her doorbell.

Anyone watching him from the street would have assumed he was crazy, Connor thought.

And maybe he was, he conceded as he finally made contact with her doorbell and pressed it.

The chiming sound seemed to vibrate in his chest, mocking him.

Time froze until he saw the door open.

And then there she was, Brianna, standing in the doorway. He watched as a myriad of emotions passed over her face in the space of a few seconds.

And then she recovered, clearing her throat. "Um, I was beginning to think that you had decided to pursue another route in tracking down your target."

"I was just looking into a few things that didn't wind up panning out," Connor said, telling her the first thing that came to his mind.

Since Brianna was still standing, blocking the doorway, he nodded toward the inside of her house. "Can I come in?"

"What?" Realizing that she was standing in his way like a statue, she snapped to life. "Oh sure. Of course." Painfully aware of how awkward she had to sound to Connor, Brianna turned away from him and led the way back to her office. "I've been looking into some of the other names," she told him.

"Even though I wasn't here?" he questioned. He

found himself looking at her, puzzled. What kind of a woman was she? "I mean, I didn't call you about not coming over yesterday. Given the so-called family record," he said, thinking of Charlotte, "you would have been within your rights to think I was guilty of pulling a disappearing act."

Now that he'd raised the point, she wanted it clarified. "Why didn't you call?" she wanted to know.

There was no actual good reason he could give her. "I got caught up in something," he answered evasively.

It was the shakiest of lies, but telling a woman you were trying to keep your distance from her didn't sound like the best way to go, either, especially now that he really wanted to put all that behind him.

Brianna nodded, as if accepting the flimsy excuse. "Well, I didn't have anything to work on at the moment and no one called me yesterday to fill in, so I thought I might as well just continue hunting for any information on those missing family members," she explained.

He couldn't see someone as busy as Brianna not having anything to do.

"You mean the dynamic duo didn't manage to run you ragged yesterday?" he asked. As soon as the words were out of his mouth, he glanced out to the hallway, expecting the children to appear. They didn't. "Speaking of which, where is my welcoming committee?" he asked Brianna. "I haven't seen or heard them since I walked in a whole five minutes ago." He stepped out into the hall to look around, but he didn't see either one of them. "They usually come charging out by now."

"Well, if they're charging out, it's at Joey and Debbie's house, not mine." She smiled to herself, thinking how both of her children had pleaded with her to let them go. It was starting. Her children were beginning to grow up. Before she knew it, they'd be getting married and leaving. The prospect of an empty nest was not all that far away, and she felt sad.

"Joey and Debbie?" he repeated, unfamiliar with the names Brianna had just mentioned.

"Friends from the park," she explained. "Their poor, brave mother—my babysitter, Beth—and her husband are hosting a slumber party for them at their house tonight."

He didn't care how brave the other woman was, he was concerned about Axel and Ava. "Aren't they a little young to be going to a slumber party?" he asked. The second the words were out, he realized that he was making noises like a parent, but the truth of it was he *didn't* think they were old enough to attend a slumber party. What had Brianna been thinking? "How many kids are going to be there?"

"Counting my two and her two?" Brianna asked. When he nodded, she answered, "Four. Beth thought she'd start out small and see how it goes. I'll probably have to wind up reciprocating." She could hear her children pleading for a slumber party of their own already. "But not until I finish working on your project."

Picking up a folder, she looked at him. "Any questions?"

"Yes. How can you stand it?" he asked her, gesturing around him to indicate the rest of the house. He was only half kidding. "It's so quiet."

She paused for a moment, cocking her head as if listening.

"It is, isn't it?" Brianna agreed. "I forgot what this could be like, working without having the walls shake every fifteen, twenty minutes." The awkwardness behind them and having slipped back into a comfortable groove with Connor again, she said, "Shall we get started?"

The next four hours were spent following up on the lead that Brianna had managed to find, plus discovering information on another person on the list along the way. The latter had happened almost by accident.

Verifications were made as well as plans to follow up with a phone call and eventually, hopefully, a face-to-face meeting.

It was all beginning to fall into place.

Leaning back in her chair, Brianna looked rather satisfied with their joint effort.

"All in all, I think we've had a very productive afternoon," she told Connor. She rotated her shoulders. They had begun to ache.

"Afternoon?" he echoed, glancing at his watch. "It's almost evening. I didn't realize we've been at this for so long," he admitted.

"I guess I can get a lot done when I'm not rushing out to check into screams and crashes every few minutes," she said with a smile. "Are you hungry?" she asked suddenly, turning toward him.

"You don't have to make dinner," Connor told her. She'd worked almost harder than he had today. He didn't want her going to any extra trouble now on his account.

Brianna waved away his protest. Besides, she wasn't making anything from scratch.

"How do you feel about leftovers?" she asked. "I made meat loaf yesterday and it's not exactly the kids' favorite."

Right now, he was hungry enough to eat the pan the meat loaf had been made in, although he kept that to himself.

"Meat loaf sounds great," Connor answered, then added, "But just so you know, I would have settled for peanut butter and jelly. Or just peanut butter," he told her.

She laughed, trying to picture him eating a peanut butter and jelly sandwich. She really couldn't. "You know, for a man of your background, you don't have very expensive tastes."

Connor wasn't sure he followed her. "My background?" he questioned.

Maybe she should explain, Brianna thought. "I said I had time on my hands. I spent part of that doing a little background research on you," she confessed. "Fortunado Real Estate—you're part of that, aren't you?" she asked, citing the real estate company that he'd told her had experienced a severe downturn.

What was she getting at? he wondered. "I didn't try to hide that," he pointed out.

"No, you didn't," she agreed, then explained her thinking. "But you showed me your private investigator credentials and a private investigator isn't the first thing that comes to mind when someone thinks of Fortunado Real Estate."

For a second he thought she was going to withhold any further information until he agreed to up her payment. He'd been dealing with people who were only out for themselves for too long.

But he knew better. Brianna wasn't like that.

Relaxing, he asked, "Is this your way of saying that your offer of meat loaf is off the table?"

Rather than go on explaining why she'd decided to look into his background and wind up embarrassing herself, she decided that the safest thing to do was just to feed him.

"Come with me," Brianna told him, taking hold of his hand.

"To the ends of the world," he quipped, then added, "Or the kitchen, whichever is first."

She laughed, dropping his hand. "You're crazy. You know that, don't you?"

He took no offense, knowing she didn't intend any. "I usually play with the kids to use up any excess energy I might have. They're not here so I guess you get to see this side of me. I can usually keep it hidden," he added with a straight face.

"Uh-huh."

Brianna warmed up what was left of the meat loaf in the microwave, then put the platter on the table. A serving of corn and leftover mashed potatoes accompanied the main dish.

Connor set the table for them as she warmed the meal. He'd been here often enough now to know where everything was kept and taking part in the domestic scene felt right. It made him uneasy that this came to him so effortlessly. This wasn't the self-image he had of himself. Why wasn't he running for his life?

"Much better than peanut butter and jelly," he commented, sitting down when she did.

She noted that he had set the table and smiled her thanks.

"They asked about you, you know. Yesterday, when you didn't come, the kids asked about you," Brianna explained. "They wanted to know what I'd done to chase you away."

He'd just taken a bite of the meat loaf and had to wait until he swallowed before asking, "What did you tell them?"

She thought of being confronted by the duo. Both had been deadly serious. "That you were a busy man and had other things to do besides working on a project here."

"Did that satisfy them?" he asked as he continued eating. His mind was hardly on the food. She'd stirred his curiosity with her story. And his libido with her nearness.

"No," Brianna said with a sigh. "They were convinced that I'd done something to make you stay away."

He waited for a couple of minutes before quietly saying, "Well, in a way, you could say that the two pipsqueaks were right."

Brianna looked up sharply at him. "I *did* do something to make you stay away?" she asked him, even though, in the back of her mind, a little voice had answered that very question yesterday, undermining her confidence. She'd managed to squelch the voice but here he was saying the same thing. "What?" she wanted to know. "What did I do to suddenly make you stay away?"

He paused, debating the wisdom of what he was about to say.

And then he said it.

"You were you."

Brianna frowned. "That makes no sense."

He didn't see it that way. "It does when I'm struggling to do the honorable thing, to stay away from you the way I promised."

"I didn't ask you to stay away," she denied. "I just asked you not to..." *Kiss me.* At a loss as to how to phrase it, Brianna found herself searching for words.

"Yeah, about that..." Connor reached over and cupped her cheek, trying his best to stifle feelings that were threatening to overwhelm him. "I can't. I can't stay away," he admitted. "I wasn't following up other leads yesterday," he confessed. "I was listing all the reasons why I should keep my distance from you. All the reasons why I should just go away." It had actually been a consideration. One he couldn't follow through on. "There was just one reason why I couldn't."

She nodded, guessing at the reason. "Because you wanted to find Charlotte."

"The hell with finding Charlotte," he said. Didn't Brianna understand what he was trying to tell her? "I couldn't go away because I couldn't get myself to leave you. To walk away and never see you again."

She had another theory about that. A far more common one.

"Maybe you can't leave because I turned you down. Probably no woman has ever said no to you before and it's a classic case of wanting something you can't have," she guessed.

"No," Connor insisted, "this is different." He saw the look that came into her eyes. "Don't worry, I'm not going to try to change your mind. I understand why you're telling me no and I respect your choice." Even though it was killing him, he added silently, "I just wanted you to know that despite everything that's currently going on in my life and despite trying to track down this woman who's trying to bring down my entire family, you were all I kept thinking about these last twenty-four hours. I couldn't get myself to focus on anything else."

She had what she wanted, Brianna thought. He was telling her that he wasn't going to try to get her to change her mind, wasn't going to try to seduce her, and she believed him. Once this project was completed, she could send Connor off and that would be that. She would be home free.

The hell she would be!

Getting up from the table, she stood beside Connor and pulled him up to his feet with her. Before he could ask her what she was doing or even say another word, Brianna threw her arms around his neck and brought her mouth up to his.

The kiss took him completely by surprise and totally incinerated every single word he had just said to her. All his noble intentions and promises just vanished into the night air as if they had never existed.

"Was it something I said?" he murmured against her lips even as he kissed her back.

"Shut up," was the only thing Brianna said before she utterly surrendered to what she had known since he had kissed her that first time was inevitable.

Her destiny.

Since she had dropped all the barriers she had so carefully constructed and diligently kept in place since Jonny had left her, Brianna expected Connor to lose no time in taking her, in uniting their bodies and satisfying the urges that she knew had to be consuming him.

She was completely surprised when instead of doing that, Connor took his time and made love to her instead. The experience was still fiery, but at the same time, his lovemaking was slow, deliberate, making her feel cherished and beautiful with every movement, every thrilling caress he delivered.

Instead of tearing off her clothes and throwing his own aside in a mad, overwhelming rush to consummate their union, Connor kissed her.

Slowly.

Deliberately.

He kissed her lips, her throat, her shoulders, sending shivers through her whole body with each touch of his mouth. His lips skimmed over each and every part of her that was exposed to him.

Somehow, although she wasn't totally aware of how, her clothes kept vanishing, allowing him to press his lips against more and more of her.

Claiming more and more of her.

She'd never made love like this before, never felt this mounting frenzy building within her before, turning her into this insatiable creature she didn't even recognize. She wasn't a shy, shrinking violet anymore. She was a woman possessed with a desire to give pleasure as well as receive it.

Somehow, without any conscious thought, she and

Connor made their way from the kitchen into the living room.

They never reached the bedroom.

It seemed as if it was leagues away and she felt demands vibrating through her body *now*.

But first she wanted Connor to remember tonight, to know that he made love with *her*, not just another one of the women she was certain passed through his life. Brianna suddenly wanted to leave her mark on his soul. Years from now, after another score of women had come and gone, she wanted him to remember this night.

To remember *her*.

She went with her instincts, some innate force he had woken up within her, and made love to Connor with the same verve and intensity that he had been making love with her.

Breathing heavily, their bodies gleaming with sweat, they finally began the last leg of this wondrous journey that was still before them.

With his eyes on hers and their hands laced together, Connor entered her.

Brianna used the last ounce of her energy to match him movement for movement, causing the sensation to swell and rush up, catching both of them in the last wave that pushed them all the way to the top.

Clinging to one another, they allowed the tide to come and carry them away.

Chapter Thirteen

"I guess it's a good thing the kids went to that sleepover," Brianna murmured.

She was curled up against Connor on the sofa. Euphoria was slowly settling in, taking the place of the wildly thrilling thunderbolts of desire that had all but done her in. She smiled as she ran her hand along his hair. "Otherwise, this might have been a little hard to explain."

"No, it wouldn't," Connor contradicted. "Because if Axel and Ava hadn't gone to that sleepover, this wouldn't have happened," he informed her, turning so that he could look into her face. He cradled her closer to him, their naked bodies touching, sending out renewed signals of longing. "At least, not until they were asleep and we were in your room with the door closed."

His response surprised her. It also warmed her.

"That's a very responsible approach," she told him, amazed that he would think of that. She'd just assumed that Connor would have put his own needs ahead of the children, especially since they weren't his and in all likelihood, he wouldn't be seeing them much longer.

"Why do you look so surprised?" he asked, brushing the back of his hand against her face, caressing her. "I'm not exactly a charging bull moose in heat."

Unable to hold herself in check, she started to laugh then, her body brushing up against his on the sofa. "I never thought of you as a bull moose, charging or otherwise," she confessed, tickled by the image he'd created.

He wasn't insulted by the reference he'd just made. "There's one thing to be said about a bull moose, though. It has great staying power."

Her brow furrowed as she frowned. "You're making that up."

Connor's expression gave nothing away. "Maybe," he allowed. Raising himself up on his elbow, he looked into her eyes. "Why don't we take this into your bedroom and see? Your sofa did in a pinch, but it's not all that comfortable."

"You didn't seem as if you were all that uncomfortable," she reminded him, amused.

"You'd be surprised how much more accommodating I can be with a little more space to work in," he told her, the look in his eyes pulling her in.

Exciting her.

"All right," she told him, "surprise me." Her smile was warm and inviting as Brianna started to rise to her feet.

Standing already, the first thing Connor did was literally sweep Brianna off her feet and into his arms.

She felt as if her very breath had whooshed out of her lungs. "What are you doing?" she squealed.

"Surprising you," Connor answered, satisfaction curving the corners of his mouth. Then he added, "I aim to please."

Brianna tucked her arms around his neck to secure herself.

"You've already taken care of that part," she told him, her eyes dancing as she thought of the last hour they had spent together.

"In the words of Al Jolson—" he began, only to be interrupted.

"Who?" she asked him. She had no idea who he was referring to.

"A famous old vaudeville showman," Connor explained.

"Vaudeville." Brianna shook her head. The man was turning out to be a walking font of information. "You are an endless source of surprises."

He laughed, then continued. "As I was about to say, in the words of the immortal Al Jolson, 'You ain't seen nothin' yet,'" Connor told her.

And it was a promise that he definitely intended to live up to.

This time, Brianna felt her heart pounding so hard when they finally fell back against her bed, she didn't know if it would ever be able to slow down to normal again. If the first time they made love had been wonderful, the second time absolutely defied all description.

It took several minutes for the room to stop spinning and several more for her body temperature to even begin to return to normal.

In all honesty, she was surprised that they hadn't set the bed on fire.

"I'm not sure," she murmured to Connor, "but I think I just died."

"I'll check you for a pulse once I get my oomph back," Connor promised. "You really wore me out. I guess it must have been all that stored-up, leftover energy you had because you didn't have to chase after your kids today."

Right now, Brianna wasn't sure if she would ever be able to move again. "Just trying to keep up with you."

"Funny, I was going to say the same thing," Connor told her. He stopped for a moment, listening. "And now I'm hearing bells," he said. "You've had some effect on me."

"That's the phone, silly," Brianna said, identifying the sound.

She turned her head toward the landline on her nightstand.

He raised his head to get a better look at the intrusive object. "That's right. I forgot you had a landline. *Why* do you have a landline?" he asked. Most people he knew didn't own one of those things these days.

"In case the electricity goes out and I can't charge my cell phone," she told him. "My line of work depends on my being reached."

She was tempted to let the landline go on ringing.

It couldn't be a potential client on the other end of the line, not at nine thirty at night.

But by the third ring, her concern that it could have something to do with the children overcame her. "I guess I'd better get that. Whoever it is probably won't go away until I answer."

With what she felt was her very last shred of energy, Brianna reached over and picked up the receiver. Bringing it up against her ear, she murmured an exceedingly tired "Hello?"

The next second, Connor saw her bolt upright. She was holding on to the receiver with both hands. "What?" she cried.

Connor sat up beside her. He had no idea what was going on, but whatever it was, he could see that it was distressing Brianna.

"What is it?" he asked. And then it came to him. There was only one thing that could get this sort of a reaction from her. "Is it one of the kids?" he wanted to know.

Brianna held her hand up, asking for silence as she continued listening to the voice on the other end of the line.

"All right, I'll be right there," she finally said, then hung up the phone.

"What is it?" Connor asked her the second that she ended the call.

"Axel threw up." He'd been so eager to go, even more so than his sister. And now she had to go and bring him home. She felt awful for the poor kid.

"Flu?" Connor asked, saying the first thing that occurred to him.

He tried to remember if flu season was over yet. He vaguely remembered hearing something on the radio during one of his drives here, but couldn't recall anything beyond that.

"Candy," Brianna answered. When Connor looked at her, confused, she explained. "Seems that besides dinner, my son decided to stuff himself with as much candy and as many snacks as he could get his hands on. Then they played some kind of game involving spinning and, well, you can imagine the rest."

"Poor kid," Connor commented.

"Poor kid?" she echoed as she walked into the living room where they'd both left their clothes. She knew why she felt that way, but what had prompted Connor to say that?

"Well, sure," he told her, collecting his clothing and quickly getting dressed. "This isn't the way he would have wanted to remember his first night away from home. It's kind of embarrassing for him."

She fully understood that, but as Axel's mother, she had a job to do. "That's nothing compared to the lecture he's going to get. He knows he's not supposed to stuff himself with that kind of garbage, especially not before bedtime."

"That's probably why he did it," Connor pointed out. "Because you weren't there to police him. Face it, you have a typical boy on your hands."

"Right now, I'd welcome him being a little less typical," Brianna answered, pulling on her jeans.

"This is harmless. Go easy on him," Connor advised. She detected a note of sympathy in his voice.

"Right now, the guy's pretty miserable and he feels bad about having to come home."

She relented. She hadn't been all that hell-bent to deliver that lecture anyway. "Maybe you're right," Brianna agreed.

Finding her purse, she began hunting through it for her car keys.

Connor put his hand out for the keys. "I'll drive," he offered.

It took her a moment for his words to register. "What?"

"Give me the address and I'll drive you," Connor told her. "We'll use your car because you have their car seats," he added.

He seemed to have thought this all out, Brianna realized. That he had really surprised her. "You're not going home?" she asked.

"I figure that Axel's going to need a guy in his corner. I'm sure Ava's probably filling in for you right now, reading him the riot act for doing something she no doubt considers dumb. With both of you there, the poor guy'll feel outnumbered. I just thought I'd offer him a little moral support."

Then, as if he knew what she was thinking, Connor added, "It's still early. Any other time, we might still be working on those names Charlotte had you looking for."

He knew she was worried about the way this looked, she thought. But he was right. On all counts. She was just being self-conscious. The kids were too young to think that anything was going on between them.

Don't get used to this.

If she did, it would be all too easy for her to start leaning on him. Depending on him.

And looking forward to his being there beside her in bed.

You know that's not how this is all going to play out, she silently insisted. *The man's here today. He's not making any commitments about tomorrow.*

Brianna took a breath, looking at him. "You sure you want to do this?"

Connor didn't answer her question, not directly. Instead, all he said was, "Let's go," and led the way out of her house to her car.

Brianna followed, focused on getting to her son.

"I'm really sorry about this," Brianna said, wholeheartedly apologizing to Beth Wilson, the mother who had called her.

"Don't worry about it," Beth told her, waving away the apology. She seemed to genuinely mean the words. "It's my fault. I shouldn't have put out all those snacks, but this was the first sleepover the kids have ever had and Joey kept saying that Axel and Ava liked all these different things." She smiled ruefully at her mistake. "I guess I didn't realize that he was eating so much." She looked down at Axel and it was obvious that she really was sorry. "Do you feel any better?"

Axel shook his head. He just looked really miserable, like he never wanted to see another piece of chocolate again.

Connor stooped down and scooped the boy up in his arms. Axel put his head against Connor's shoulder. "You'll feel better in the morning, big guy," Connor promised.

The woman hosting the children's slumber party looked at Connor with unabashed appreciation, her eyes traveling up and down the length of him.

"You're not their father, are you?" she asked.

Brianna felt that it was time to step in and she placed herself between Beth and Connor as he held her little boy.

"This is Connor Fortunado, a client," she told the other mother. "We were working on some files when you called about Axel's mishap."

"Working," Beth repeated, drawing the single word out with a wide smile. "I see." Then, touching Axel's arm, the woman said, "I hope you feel better, dear. We'll have you both back when you've recovered from this," she promised the little boy, looking at Ava, as well.

"Can't he stay, Mom?" Joey asked. Six months older than his friend, he was clearly unhappy to have the evening end so abruptly.

"Not tonight, I'm afraid, honey," Beth told him. She walked the foursome to the front door. Joey and his sister, Debbie, trailed after them. "It was nice meeting you, Mr. Fortunado," Beth made a point of saying to Connor.

Brianna caught the interested, friendly note in the woman's voice. She couldn't really blame her, Brianna supposed. Connor was certainly a great deal more handsome than the average man.

"Again, I'm sorry about this," Brianna apologized one last time for her son.

Beth waved her hand, although her attention was still partially divided. "Don't give it another thought. Bye." Then she added almost wistfully, "Enjoy the rest of your evening."

"You know what she's thinking," Brianna said to Connor in a low voice as they opened the car doors.

Even so, Ava managed to overhear her. "What's she thinking, Mama?" the little girl asked.

"That she's sorry the two of you had to leave so early," Connor told her, saving Brianna from having to come up with an answer.

"I didn't have to leave," Ava informed them with a pout. "*I* didn't throw up," she added almost accusingly. "Axel did."

Normally Axel would have spoken up in his own defense at this point. Most likely he would have offered up a denial or come up with something to throw back in his sister's face. But this time, all the boy did was moan.

"You still feeling sick, big guy?" Connor asked sympathetically. "Do you think you're going to throw up again?"

The miserable look on the little boy's pale, freckled face told Connor that the answer was a definite yes.

"Tell you what, why don't I sit in the back with you to make sure you don't wind up throwing up on your sister?" Connor suggested.

Both of the car seats were in the back. He figured he'd just sit between them.

Whoa, Connor thought. What was he doing? He was getting in way too deep here with these kids. As soon as Brianna got them home, he needed to put on the skids. Otherwise, there would be no getting out and he could just kiss his carefree life goodbye. Permanently.

The idea of her brother throwing up on her horrified Ava. "I don't wanna sit with Axel!" she wailed indignantly.

"You won't be," Connor assured her. "You'll be next to me. I'll be sitting between you and your brother. If he starts to throw up again, I'll turn his head away so that it'll land on this old blanket." He pointed to the blanket he'd folded up and tucked against the door next to the boy.

Ava walked over to the blanket he'd indicated. "Oh." Satisfied that she would be out of the line of fire, she nodded. "Okay," she agreed, circling back to her side of the vehicle. She waited for Connor to put her into her car seat.

"Here're your keys back." He offered them to Brianna, then heard himself saying, "I'll get the kids into their seats."

He had to stop doing that, he thought. But then, this was just for a little while longer. And then he'd be gone, right?

About to tell him that she would take care of strapping her children in, Brianna stopped and let Connor take over.

He'd be gone soon enough and she might as well enjoy this now, while it lasted.

He was right to insist on coming, Brianna thought, despite the fact that his presence had given Beth Wilson something to think about and most likely to talk about. There was really no way she could have handled

Axel in his present condition and still driven the children home. Ava would have voiced her displeasure in a high, loud voice all the way home.

This was all a lot easier with Connor, she thought, finally getting in on the driver's side.

Everything was a lot easier with Connor around.

You have to stop doing that. This is temporary. Just temporary. If she allowed herself to get used to this, it was going to be twice as hard on her when he left. And he *would* leave. She just needed to remember that.

"Everything all right, Bri?" Connor asked, breaking into her thoughts. "You haven't started the car," he pointed out.

Bri. He called her Bri. As if they were a couple. Her heart melted.

Stop that! she silently upbraided herself.

"As fine as it can be with one nauseous little boy in the backseat," she answered.

"I'm sorry, Mommy," Axel bleated.

Her heart went out to him. "You'll feel better soon. But just remember how you feel the next time you want to eat everything in sight," she told him.

"I will," Axel said meekly.

This time, Brianna started up the car.

Chapter Fourteen

The minute Brianna parked her car in her driveway, Connor got out and came around to Axel's car seat. Undoing the restraints, he was careful to gently pick the boy up and take him into his arms.

Walking behind Brianna, who had her daughter by the hand, Connor carried Axel to the room the boy shared with his sister. After helping Axel wash his face and hands and changing him into his pajamas, Connor asked him, "Which is your bed?"

"He sleeps in the top bunk," Ava announced, coming back into the bedroom once Connor walked back in with her brother.

There was a problem with that tonight, Connor thought. He exchanged looks with Brianna. "And the bottom bunk is yours?" he asked the little girl.

"Uh-huh." Ave bobbed her head up and down, confirming her response.

"How about, just for tonight, you let your brother have the bottom bunk?" Connor suggested.

"But why?" Ava wanted to know, her eyes widening.

"If he feels sick again during the night, Axel will be able to get to the bathroom faster if he's in the bottom bunk. Besides, you don't want to have him suddenly throw up while he's up there, do you? It could get pretty messy down here for you," Connor warned, eyeing her closely.

He felt he had made a winning argument, but one look at Ava's face told him that they weren't home free yet. Ava appeared to be totally distressed. "But I'm afraid of top bunks," she told Connor.

"Ava's afraid of heights," Brianna explained. "That's why I gave her the bottom bunk." She looked at her daughter. There was only one way out of this without a squabble. "Tell you what, how would you like to spend the night in my bed?"

"I won't fall out?" Ava asked uncertainly, looking up at her mother with wide eyes.

Brianna smiled. This was familiar territory. Ava was never going to be a daredevil. "No, you won't fall out, sweetheart. I won't let you," she added to reassure her.

"Okay," Ava agreed, although she still sounded rather reluctant.

"Problem solved," Connor pronounced with a wide grin, looking at Brianna.

"You're getting really good with them," Brianna

told him. She didn't bother to keep the pleased note out of her voice.

"It's simple. I just watched you," Connor said, shrugging off any credit.

Brianna turned toward her daughter. "Ava, why don't you stay with your brother for a few minutes while I walk Mr. Fortunado out? When I come back, I'll get you ready for bed," she told the little girl.

Ava brightened immediately. Brianna knew that the little girl liked the idea of being put in charge of her older brother. Ava liked being the boss.

"Okay, Mama," she replied.

Her obedient tone wasn't fooling anyone, Brianna thought fondly. First chance she got, Ava would be ordering her brother around.

Ruffling the little girl's silky hair, Brianna told her daughter, "I'll be right back."

"Good night, half-pint," Connor said to the little girl, then he turned toward the very unhappy-looking little boy lying listlessly in the bottom bunk. "Feel better, big guy."

Rather than saying anything, Axel moaned in response.

"How come I'm a half-pint and he's a big guy?" Ava wanted to know. She obviously thought that the word *big* was complimentary in this case.

Brianna patted the small, dark head. "I'll explain it all later, honey," she promised, hoping to buy herself a little time to come up with an answer. Then, turning toward Connor, she said, "Let's go."

"Yes, ma'am," he answered obediently. When they

reached the front door, Connor commented, "Some night, eh?"

"Well, you can say that again. At the very least, it's certainly been an eventful one," she agreed. And then she smiled up at him, grateful he'd been there with her. "Thanks for all your help," she told him. "It wouldn't have gone nearly as smoothly without you there."

He looked at her for a second, and then seemed to understand her meaning. "Oh, you're talking about with the kids. Sure. It wouldn't have been right just to leave you high and dry, having to cope with a sick kid and all," he told her.

"My ex-boyfriend had no qualms about doing that," Brianna recalled, addressing his last comment first. "And of course I'm talking about help with the kids. As for the other part of this evening," she said, referring to making love with Connor, "that's something that we *don't* need to talk about."

It struck him that she was highly unusual. A woman who *didn't* want to take apart and dissect the meaning behind every nuance, every action that had taken place during their lovemaking.

He looked at her for a long moment, impressed. "You are in a class by yourself, Brianna Childress," he said just before he bent over and kissed her.

In a strange, ironic sort of way, Connor thought, he had Charlotte Robinson to thank for this. For bringing Brianna into his life. Not by design, but certainly by happy accident.

He had a feeling finding this out would *not* be well received by the woman. Connor suppressed a pleased smile.

"I'll see you tomorrow," Brianna said, waiting for him to verify her statement. She would be lying if she said that she didn't live with the specter of Connor leaving permanently in the near future.

Connor nodded. "And I promise I won't bring any ice cream or cookies for Axel and Ava."

"Axel'll probably be ready to eat them by tomorrow," Brianna predicted about her son. "But don't," she cautioned just in case Connor was having any second thoughts about what he'd just promised.

A smile played on his lips as he gave Brianna a little salute, touching two fingers to his temple like a soldier.

But before he could say goodbye, Ava's voice was suddenly heard calling, sounding high-pitched and insistent. "Mama, Axel's going to be sick again."

"Go, go!" Connor told her, although the words were rather needless since he addressed them to Brianna's back. She was already hurrying to the children's bedroom. "Good luck," Connor murmured as he pulled the door closed behind him.

He heard the lock click into place. Satisfied, he walked to his car. He still had to drive home, he reminded himself, and admittedly, he was rather tired.

But thoughts of making love with Brianna kept him wide-awake all the way home.

"So, how is he?" Connor asked Brianna when he arrived at her house the following day.

It was almost noon. He would have been there earlier, but he'd actually been busy taking care of some extraneous details, all of which had kept him from driving over here first thing in the morning.

Although it hadn't kept him from thinking about making love with Brianna the entire time.

"Like it never happened," Brianna answered his question, opening the door all the way for him. The resilience of children never ceased to amaze her. "Come see for yourself," she said, inviting Connor in. "He's asking for a do-over."

"A do-over?" Connor questioned, puzzled.

"Yes, he wants to go over to Joey's house for another sleepover tonight. I told him it wasn't happening, at least not for a while. He's not happy about the news," she added. "But he'll get used to it," she said philosophically.

Connor nodded. Instead of going into the children's bedroom, he suddenly asked her a question out of the blue, "Can you get a babysitter?"

The question caught her completely off guard. Brianna looked at him quizzically, then slowly told Connor, "I guess so. For when and for how long?" she wanted to know. She couldn't make any sort of plans without that information.

"This Saturday," Connor answered. "And as for how long, that's anyone's guess."

That wasn't exactly helpful, she thought. "You're going to have to be a little more specific than that."

"I've been invited to a baby shower," he told her. Then, before she could point out the obvious, Connor added, "It's a coed baby shower. They're all the thing these days."

They might be all the "thing," she thought, but she wouldn't know anyone there and she was rather shy. "I don't think—"

He didn't want her to say no. He wasn't about to analyze why, but it was suddenly important to him that she come with him, if for no other reason than she see some of the people she had been researching.

"It's a family affair," he told her, then specified, "A *big* family affair. Some of the people I've been trying to locate may be there, along with a lot of other members who I already know." He'd met some of them a few months ago when his sister Schuyler had organized a family reunion. "I thought you might like to meet some of the names you encountered during your initial research for Charlotte."

He was tempting her.

Everything seemed different to her now that she'd made love with him. She found herself *wanting* to meet his family.

"Well, I have to admit that I am kind of curious about them," she confessed.

He couldn't have been more pleased. "Great, it's all settled," he declared happily.

It didn't quite work that way, she thought.

"Hello, mother of two," she reminded him, waving a hand before his eyes as if that helped underscore her point. "Nothing's settled until I can make arrangements to leave the kids with someone."

"You're leaving us?" Ava cried, clearly horror-stricken. Neither one of them had seen the little girl come into the doorway of the living room. "It's 'cause Axel threw up, isn't it?" she asked her mother, then whirled around on her heel, turning toward her room, where she'd left her brother. "Axel, you're making Mama go away."

Brianna sighed as she shook her head. "Never a dull moment," she said to Connor.

Axel stumbled into the living room, still somewhat unsteady after last night's episode.

Connor quickly took over. "Hey, guys, your mother's not leaving you. You know better than that. She'd never leave you. She's just going to get someone to stay with you so she can go to a party for a few hours," he explained to them.

"You're fibbing," Ava accused. "Mama doesn't go to parties," she insisted. "She just goes to work. Sometimes to the store."

"You went to a party," Connor reminded the small, judgmental audience. "Don't you think your mom should have a chance to do that, too?"

Ava looked as if she was really thinking the question over. Axel took the momentary lull as his chance to speak up. Drawing closer to Connor, he eagerly asked, "Can you be the one to babysit us?"

This was getting out of hand again, Brianna thought. So what else was new?

"Axel, Ava, stop putting Mr. Fortunado on the spot," she told them.

"I would," Connor said, interrupting Brianna and answering the little boy's question. "But I'm the one taking her to the party."

"Can you take us, too?" Ava wanted to know, looking at him hopefully.

"Okay, you two," Brianna said, her voice growing serious now. "I think you both need to stop bothering Mr. Fortunado and just be grateful for everything he's done for you so far."

"Like what?" Ava wanted to know. The little girl wasn't trying to be wise, she was really asking for an example.

"Like helping to bring you home last night," Brianna answered. "Like bringing over pizza for you to eat. Like playing games with you two," she enumerated, looking from one child to the other.

A light seemed to dawn on Axel. "Oh. Yeah. That," he remembered, hanging his head.

"Yes, 'that,'" Brianna echoed. Her annoyance spent, she said, "Now why don't you two go play with Muffin and Scruffy for a while? Mr. Fortunado and I have work to do," she told them.

But apparently Ava had more questions for her mother. "Why do you call him that?" she wanted to know, glancing toward Connor as she asked her mother.

Brianna knew her daughter. Ava wasn't stalling. She appeared to really want to know the answer to her question.

"Mr. Fortunado?" Brianna repeated. Ava's head went up and down. "Because that's his name," she told the little girl.

Ava knew that, but it apparently didn't answer her question. "Don't you like him?" she asked.

"Yes, I like him," Brianna said. She avoided looking at Connor as she said it.

"Then why don't you call him Connor?" Ava wanted to know. "That's his name." The little girl smiled at him. "He likes being called Connor."

Why was everything a struggle with these two, Brianna wondered. A struggle and a debate. "All right. If

I call him Connor, will you and your brother go back in your room and play?"

"Sure!" the two cried, united for the space of exactly a moment. Even so, the children remained where they were.

Brianna frowned. "Well? Why aren't you going to your room to play?"

Ava exchanged looks with her brother. It was clear that for now, she was the spokesman. "'Cause we're waiting for you to call him Connor," Ava answered.

Brianna tamped down her annoyance. "Let's get to work, *Connor*," she said.

And just like that, her children grinned and took off.

Connor, she noted, had been struggling to keep a straight face. Now that her children were gone, he gave up the effort.

"I think," Connor said, laughing, "if they gave out medals for mothers, I'd definitely nominate you to get one."

"Thank you," she murmured. She debated her next words, then told him, "I'm just grateful that you're not making a run for the hills. That you didn't make a run for it the first day you heard my two arguing with each other at the top of their lungs," she admitted.

She was serious, he realized. In all fairness, ordinarily he would have been that guy. But there was something about this woman that got to him from the first moment she mistook him for the plumber and grabbed his hand, pulling him into her house.

"They're entertaining," Connor told her as they went to her office.

"Their dad didn't think so," Brianna murmured, more to herself than to him.

Connor slanted a look at her as they sat down, wondering if he should say anything. He didn't want to insult Brianna and he certainly didn't want to say anything that would make her back off.

But he owed her honesty, he decided, and he did feel strongly about this point. "No offense, but their dad was an idiot."

"None taken," she assured Connor with a humorless laugh. And then she added, "And between the two of us, yes, he was."

Now that she had pushed open the door, Connor had more questions for her. "How long were the two of you together?"

Brianna was quiet for so long, he thought she was going to ignore the question. And then she said, "Five years."

Five years seemed like an awfully long time to spend with someone who was obviously so self-centered. "Why did you stay?"

Brianna debated coming up with excuses. But there really was no point in making anything up. So she was honest with him.

"I guess I'm just a sucker for strays. I kept thinking I could help him, turn him around so that he could be the father the kids deserved." She pressed her lips together, remembering. "Jonny had a substance abuse problem and I thought that if I could just say the right thing, find the right way to approach his problem, I could help him kick the habit. Help him become a better person." She laughed at herself.

It was a sad sound, Connor thought.

"You can't change anyone, Bri, no matter how good

your intentions are. They have to want to change themselves," Connor said.

"I know, you're right, but I really thought I could help," she said ruefully. "And there were the two kids we had."

"The kids he didn't want, as you said," Connor recalled.

"The kids he didn't want," Brianna repeated, confirming the truth behind those words. Brianna blew out a breath. There was no point in rehashing the past and there was work to get done. "Look, hurricanes Axel and Ava are liable to come whirling back here at any moment, so I suggest that we use this time to work on that list of names we're whittling down," she told Connor.

"Right as usual," he answered warmly. And then he paused. "But you are coming with me to the shower this Saturday, right?"

"If I can find a sitter," Brianna reminded him pointedly.

"Don't worry, you'll get a sitter even if I have to buy one for you," Connor told her.

She wasn't sure if he was kidding, but she intended to do this on her own. She didn't want him thinking of her as some helpless female. There were only so many times he could be allowed to ride to her rescue.

"Don't worry. It's not going to come to that," Brianna told him. "I have a few people who owe me favors. I'll find someone."

He nodded. "Okay. But if you don't, my offer's still open."

Connor smiled at her as he said it.

Brianna did her best not to get lost in that smile. She didn't succeed.

Chapter Fifteen

"You're not saying anything," Brianna said self-consciously.

Butterflies were madly crashing into one another in her stomach. She was already nervous that she wasn't going to fit in because the dress she'd borrowed from Beth Wilson wasn't good enough to wear to the shower that she was attending with Connor.

When she'd opened the door a minute ago to let Connor in after he'd rung her bell, he hadn't said a single word in response to her greeting.

Not even *hello*.

He was still just standing there in total silence, just looking at her.

Brianna drew the only conclusion she could from his silence. "You don't like it."

Connor finally forced himself to snap out of his trancelike state.

"Like it?" he echoed. "I *love* it. It's gorgeous. *You're* gorgeous," Connor corrected himself. For the first time in his life he felt like he was tripping over his own tongue. "I'm just trying to get used to seeing you like this. I've never seen you wearing anything but jeans and a T-shirt before."

Brianna still wasn't convinced. "So it's okay?" she asked hesitantly.

He had to laugh. "If it was any more 'okay' I wouldn't let you leave the house. I know guys aren't supposed to say things like that these days, but—wow. Just *wow*."

"*Wow* is fine." She pushed back her uncertainty and her nerves. "*Wow* is good," Brianna amended.

Connor took in a deep breath. The light scent she was wearing almost made him dizzy. *She* made him dizzy, he thought.

"Are you ready?" he asked her.

Brianna nodded as she grabbed her purse. "Just let me tell the sitter we're leaving."

At the last minute, she'd managed to get Beth Wilson's younger sister, Meredith, to stay with Ava and Axel. Meredith was getting her teaching license and wanted to be a kindergarten teacher, so she was more than happy to watch the children. She saw this as perfect training for her future vocation.

Connor stood patiently by, waiting for Brianna to say goodbye to her clinging children. He found himself reassuring them, that yes, he'd bring their mother back to them tonight.

And then finally, they were off.

"I'm really glad you're coming with me," Connor said once they were in his car and on their way to the baby shower. Admittedly, a baby shower was *not* his thing, but attending the event would allow him to get together with members of the Fortune clan he hadn't met yet. "I've never been to one of these things before and I don't want to make a fool of myself."

"A coed shower's probably different from a regular shower," Brianna told him. "I doubt if there'll be any silly games or anything like that," she told him. "So you can relax. I'm the one who's going to be out of her element." She saw him turning toward her quizzically. "I won't know anyone."

"Don't worry about it," he counseled. "I probably won't know half the people there, either. The whole idea of my going to the shower is to meet relatives I haven't met yet and to spread the word about Charlotte. To warn them about Charlotte," Connor amended.

"So they don't know that she's done all those things you told me about? The hacking and burning down your—half uncle, is it?" she asked. Connor nodded in response. "Burning down his mansion," Brianna continued. "They don't know she's the one behind it?"

It hadn't been as obvious as she thought. "I've just put the pieces together recently myself," Connor explained. "So in all likelihood, a lot of these people might not have figured it out yet. And others probably don't even know about Charlotte."

Brianna sat back in the passenger seat, thinking over what he'd just said. "This is going to be an interesting baby shower," she commented.

* * *

Truer words were never spoken, Connor thought less than half an hour later.

When they arrived at the party, most of the guests were already there. The baby shower was being thrown for a very pregnant Billie Fortune Pemberton and her husband, rodeo champion Grayson Fortune. Since this was his family's company as well as the company that had suffered recent setbacks thanks to Charlotte's devious machinations, Connor felt they were all connected to one another in a number of ways besides just by blood.

"I'm really looking forward to meeting Grayson, Nathan and Jayden Fortune," Connor confided to the woman at his side as they made their way through the room where the party was being held. The triplet brothers hadn't made it to the reunion.

Brianna found herself wishing that she had brought the notes she'd been working on for Connor. Maybe then she could keep people's names and faces straight, she thought.

"My Lord, those three look like carbon copies of each other," she whispered to Connor, spotting Grayson and his brothers.

Connor grinned. "They're triplets," he told Brianna. All three had dark brown hair and brown eyes and stood over six feet tall.

"How do their wives tell them apart?" Brianna marveled.

"I'm sure they have their ways," he answered with a wink. "Those are the sons that Gerald didn't know he fathered until recently," Connor said. "They were raised by their single mother, Deborah."

Right now, he didn't remember how much Brianna knew and how much of this information he'd discovered for himself before he'd come to her. Repeating the information drove it home for him.

"Once Gerald finally found out about them, that's when he finally left Charlotte. He was furious that she knew of the triplets' existence and had been keeping it from him all this time. I think she secretly knew that unlike all the other women Gerald had slept with, both as Gerald Robinson and under his first identity as Jerome Fortune, Deborah was the one woman he had always really loved. Once he found out that Deborah had given birth to his sons, he tracked her down and begged for her forgiveness."

Brianna supposed maybe there was hope for the man, after all—if he survived Charlotte's wrath, she thought. "Well, if that's the case and Charlotte is as vindictive as you said she is, why hasn't she tried to seek revenge against Deborah yet?"

She was certain they would have heard about any attempts by now. She was beginning to realize that Connor had his finger on the pulse of everything connected to the family.

"Because the woman is nothing if not crafty. She might be evil personified, but she is definitely patient when it comes to exacting her revenge," Jayden Fortune said, answering Brianna's question. The triplet had walked up behind them just in time to overhear the conversation.

After formally introducing himself and his wife,

Ariana, to both Connor and Brianna, he told them that he and his two brothers were as surprised as anyone to have Gerald suddenly show up in their lives after all these years.

"We'd never met him until then and it wasn't exactly a *warm* reunion as far as my brothers and I were concerned," Jayden told them.

"That's putting it mildly," Grayson said with a harsh laugh.

"As a matter of fact, we were ready to ride the man out on a rail," Jayden continued, "'father' or no 'father.' We all thought that he had deserted Mom as soon as he knew she was pregnant. But he swore up and down that he never knew. We all had our suspicions that his wife knew—the woman's a viper that knows *everything*," Jayden maintained, "but Charlotte would have never told him about us because she was probably afraid that Gerald would have tried to do right by our mother."

"She turned out to be right," Nathan said, joining the conversation. "And Mom," he said as he exchanged looks with his two brothers, "well, our mom has this kind, forgiving heart," he told Connor and Brianna. "And she believed Gerald when he said he never knew that she was pregnant when he left."

"She seems genuinely happy with Jerome or Gerald or whatever the hell he calls himself these days," Grayson told Connor and Brianna. "My brothers and I haven't really taken to him yet," he said honestly. "But as long as Mom's happy and he's good to her, well, that's all that really counts."

"Your wife was writing a series of articles on Gerald Robinson, wasn't she?" Connor recalled, addressing the question to Jayden.

"Yes, she was." He looked around for Ariana, who had wandered off to talk to someone else at the party. "That's how Ariana and I initially met," Jayden explained.

"I'd love to pick her brain and ask her a few questions sometime if I could," Connor told the man.

Jayden saw no reason to wait. "Now's as good a time as any." Turning toward an attractive woman who was talking to Billie, the next mother-to-be, Jayden put out his hand. "Honey, I've got someone here who wants to talk to my wife, the reporter," he told her. "Do you have a few minutes to talk shop?"

Ariana's smile was warm and relaxed. "Always," she told him. Turning toward Connor and Brianna, she asked, "What would you like to know?"

Connor didn't hesitate. "Everything."

Ariana looked mildly surprised.

"Connor here thinks that Charlotte is bent on getting revenge against the family," her husband explained.

Ariana automatically shivered at the mention of the other woman's name.

"It certainly wouldn't surprise me," the reporter told the small gathering. "I think Charlotte could probably trace her lineage back to Lucrezia Borgia."

"She hasn't poisoned anyone," Nathan's wife, Bianca, pointed out.

"Yet," Jayden said.

The others laughed, but it was an uncomfortable laugh that had an element of truth in it.

"Personally, I don't know what Mother sees in Gerald," Grayson told them. "The man cheated on Charlotte so many times he's probably lost count. I don't know how many illegitimate offspring he has. In fact, I don't think *he* knows."

"I bet Charlotte does," Jayden told the others.

This was his cue to speak up, Connor thought. "Brianna and I are trying to locate as many of those offspring as we can." He saw Bianca and Ariana look at him quizzically. "I want all of them to know that Charlotte potentially might have them in her sights. They need to be warned so she doesn't catch them off guard and wind up doing something awful to them," Connor said.

"You do know that Julius Fortune, Jerome's father, had four illegitimate sons himself," Ariana asked.

Jayden's wife seemed uncomfortable telling him that, perhaps because she didn't know how much Connor knew about the so-called family patriarch and she didn't want to be the one telling family secrets.

"Oh, I know," Connor replied, effectively negating her concern. "I even know their names." He proceeded to recite them. "There's my dad, Kenneth. There's also Miles, Gary and David," he told the small gathering. "I met Miles and his family at the family reunion in January. I haven't made contact with Gary or David or any of their families yet," he confessed, "but I'm going to see if I can get in contact with them next. Provided no other major disasters take place," he added, thinking of the estate fire that had set everything off.

"Hey, everybody," Bianca cut in, calling their attention to the front of the room. "They're bringing out the cake."

The present conversation regarding the devious Charlotte Robinson was tabled until after the gifts were opened and everyone had gotten at least one slice of the multi-tiered cake.

"So, did my family manage to overwhelm you?" Connor asked Brianna when they left the party and were finally on their way home.

"I'm not sure if *overwhelm* is the correct word here, but there certainly are a lot of them," Brianna replied with a quiet laugh.

"And there's even more." Connor smiled. He was a little overwhelmed himself. "It's kind of hard to tell all the players without a scorecard," he admitted, then sighed. "It's not exactly a Norman Rockwell painting come to life."

"Families can be messy," Brianna agreed. She tried to be kind in her assessment. "I guess parents don't always realize the kind of damage they can do to their children by their actions."

"No argument there," Connor agreed. "I didn't realize it at the time, but I'm really lucky to have grown up in a happy home with two parents who loved each other and still do."

The words were no sooner out of his mouth than Connor realized his mistake. He shouldn't have drawn attention to that. He saw Brianna wince and he knew she was thinking of her own children, who had never really had a father on the scene.

"I'm sorry. I didn't mean that the way it came out," Connor apologized.

But she waved off his guilty reaction. "There's no need to apologize," she told him. "You're right. Parenthood is a heavy responsibility and it's definitely not for everyone," Brianna said, thinking of Jonny again. He just hadn't been cut out to take care of a family.

To him they had been a burden, not a blessing.

She'd finally come to terms with that.

Connor was silent for a moment. "Do you ever regret having Ava and Axel?"

She didn't hesitate. "Not for one second of one day," Brianna told him. "Those kids are everything to me. I love them more than life itself and I'll always put them first."

They had reached her house. Connor pulled up into her driveway and turned off the ignition. Rather than get out, he shifted to face her.

"And who puts you first?" Connor asked.

Brianna had no answer for that. She'd been so busy giving and taking care of people and animals, she hadn't thought of herself. It felt that she hadn't had any alone time until Connor had showed up.

Shrugging, she looked away because the answer to his question was no one.

Connor crooked his finger beneath her chin, turning her head so that she faced him and he could look into her eyes.

"Let me be the one, Bri," he told her softly. "Let me be the one who puts you first."

It wasn't a proposal, she knew that. But it was a sign. A sign of hope.

She knew she was setting herself up, that she was as likely to be disappointed as she was to be elated, but she refused to dwell on the downside, to think that this wouldn't lead anywhere.

She had lived so long without being in love, without any hope that the future was going to turn out the way that she wanted it to, that Brianna found herself grasping not at straws, but at the mere *promise* of a straw.

For now, that was enough, and who knew? Maybe that promise, that *hope* would swell and take root, becoming something that would flower into the happiness she so desperately craved.

Craved not just for herself, but for her children, as well.

Because her children deserved to be happy and to grow up feeling loved not just by one parent but by two parents.

"You're crying," Connor realized. About to open his own door to get out, he stopped and looked at her. "Did I say something wrong?"

"No," Brianna answered, shaking her head. "No, you said something right."

He rubbed his thumb along her cheek, brushing away traces of her tears. He brought his thumb up to his lips and tasted it.

"Salty," he commented. "I need something sweet to counterbalance it." Connor leaned in closer to her, lightly taking hold of her shoulders. "I know just the thing," he whispered.

The next moment, his lips met hers. Instantly he could feel passion taking hold of him. There were no regrets over what he had said to her moments ago. He'd meant it. He wanted to take care of her. This was the woman he wanted to have in his life. The woman he felt he'd been looking for. He realized that he had done a one-eighty from the man he had been such a short while ago—and he liked it.

"Definitely sweet," he whispered just before he kissed her again.

And then, after a beat, Connor drew his head back. "We'd better go in before I get carried away," he told her. There was a twinkle in his eyes as he asked, "By the way, when are the kids going to go on another one of those sleepovers?"

The sound of her laughter returned everything to normal.

Chapter Sixteen

She was in love.

Brianna had to be honest with herself and admit the truth. Although she had tried to resist this, she had definitely fallen in love with Connor Fortunado.

Connor was spending more and more time with her and he was no longer hiding behind an excuse. He wasn't coming over because she was working for him or with him. He was coming over for the simple reason that he wanted to spend time with her, as well as with her kids. That, for her, was the cherry on the sundae.

Although Brianna told herself she needed to put the skids on, to go into this relationship slowly, she knew it was too late for that. She'd opened up her heart to this man. Connor didn't shut out her kids or pretend to put up with them when he actually secretly wanted them to be elsewhere. On the contrary, he included them. He took them along on their dinners out and let himself be pulled into the games that Ava and Axel wanted to play at home.

She knew it was still early and she shouldn't get too far ahead of herself, but it was so hard not to. So hard not to just love this man who her children adored.

"He seems like a really nice guy," Beth Wilson said to her one afternoon while their kids were playing together in the backyard. "But if you don't mind my butting in, I'd proceed slowly with him if I were you," her friend cautioned.

"Because I have an awful track record," Brianna said, guessing at the reason why Beth was attempting to warn her.

"No, because Connor might not be as committed to this relationship as you are," Beth explained. The older woman smiled at Brianna. "I just don't want to see you get hurt."

She appreciated the concern, but she wasn't going to change anything. "Until he came along, I was convinced I couldn't feel anything at all anymore. Connor woke up my heart—and it's really wonderful to be able to feel again," Brianna said with enthusiasm.

"Well, then go for it," Beth told her. "And I'll keep my fingers crossed for you—and maybe my toes, too," she added with a smile.

"Just not while you're walking," Brianna advised with a grin.

"Mama, I don't feel so good," Ava complained a couple of days later. She presented herself listlessly in front of her mother. "My hair hurts."

Brianna immediately thought of Ava's brother. Things could get physical very quickly between the siblings. "Axel, did you pull your sister's hair?" she wanted to know.

The little boy was sitting on the sofa. "No, I didn't," Axel denied indignantly. He pointed to the TV. "I was playing the video game. The dragon keeps trying to eat me," he complained.

Ordinarily, Brianna tried to limit the amount of time Axel played video games every day. But right now, her mind wasn't on video games. She was concerned about her daughter.

She turned to look at Ava. The little girl looked very pale and there was sweat pasting her hair to her forehead.

"What do you feel, baby?" she asked Ava.

The normal enthusiasm she always heard in Ava's voice was missing.

"Hot," the little girl told her in a quiet voice. "I'm hot."

"Come here, let me see." Brianna beckoned her over closer. Rather than going to get a thermometer, she decided to rely on the tried and true, old-fashioned method. She lightly pressed a kiss to the little girl's forehead. "You *are* hot," Brianna confirmed. "Stay right here."

She went to get a thermometer out of the medicine cabinet and brought it over to where Ava was slumped against the sofa. She pressed the button, bringing the thermometer to life. The word *low* flashed across the tiny screen where the numbers usually registered.

"Okay, you know how the drill goes," she told her daughter, trying to sound cheerful and turning this into a game. "Put this under your tongue," Brianna said. "Can you do that for me?"

"I can do that for you, Mom," Axel volunteered, raising his hand and waving it at her while still holding his video controller in his other hand.

"Next time, Axel," she told her son. "Right now I need to see how high Ava's fever is."

"Is it high?" Axel asked before she had even taken Ava's temperature. "Is she going to die?"

The question was jarring, but she tried to remember that he didn't really mean it the way it sounded.

"No, she's not going to die, Axel," Brianna said, doing her best to sound patient. Ava still hadn't opened up her mouth. "C'mon, baby, I need to see what your temperature is." After some more coaxing, she finally got the thermometer under Ava's tongue.

When the noise went off, she took thermometer out again.

"What is it? What is it?" Axel wanted to know, coming over and trying to see over his mother's shoulder.

Brianna knew that Ava had to be sick because she wasn't even asking what the temperature was.

"Well, you definitely have a temperature, but it's not *too* high," Brianna emphasized. A hundred wasn't too high when it came to children under seven. She'd heard that somewhere. "But I am putting you to bed, young lady."

Ava didn't protest. That *definitely* worried her.

When evening came, Brianna transferred the little girl to her bed. She didn't want Axel catching the cold she figured her daughter had.

Axel looked overjoyed to finally have his own room. "Cool. I get the whole room all to myself," the boy crowed happily.

His elated mood lasted all of half an hour before he came into Brianna's bedroom, a sheepish look on his face as he peered in.

"Mom, can I sleep here, too?"

"What about having the whole room to yourself?" Brianna asked him, surprised that he wanted to give up the temporary arrangement.

"It's too big," he finally said after a few minutes. "And it makes noises. I can hear it," he complained.

"That's just your imagination, honey." She knew that both of her kids had exceptionally vivid ones.

"My imagination makes noises, too," Axel told her solemnly.

She started to tell Axel that he needed to be brave and return to his room when Ava's breathing suddenly became labored.

Axel's head instantly whirled in his sister's direction. "Why's she breathing so funny, Mommy?" he wanted to know. For all of his blasé attitude, the little boy looked worried.

That makes two of us, Brianna thought, still trying to maintain a brave front for her children's benefit.

This time Brianna didn't bother with the thermometer again. She had already taken Ava's temperature over half a dozen times since she had brought the little girl into her room and put her to bed there.

Putting her hand against her daughter's forehead, Brianna pulled it back almost immediately. Ava's forehead felt as if it was on fire.

"Go get dressed, Axel. I'm dropping you off at Mrs. Wilson's house," Brianna told her son as she reached for the phone.

"For a sleepover?" Axel asked eagerly.

There was no point in alarming him and telling Axel the truth. "Yes. For a sleepover," she answered instead.

"Ava, too?" Axel wanted to know.

The fact that he was including his sister squeezed her heart. The phone on the other end was ringing and she was waiting for Beth to answer. "No, I'm taking Ava to the hospital."

Rather than run happily off to get ready for the sleepover, Axel stood where he was, looking at his sister. He had a sad expression on his face. "She's really sick, isn't she, Mommy?"

Rather than say yes, Brianna told her son, "The doctors'll get her well." She heard Beth pick up. "Now hurry and get dressed!"

Axel hurried out of the room.

"Don't worry about a thing," Beth told her twenty minutes later as the woman met her at the car. As she spoke, Beth took hold of Axel's hand. "Just get Ava to the emergency room. I'd come with you, but Harry's not home," she said, referring to her husband. "He's working the late shift tonight and there's no one to stay with the kids. Meredith's not answering her phone," she added, mentioning her younger sister.

"I really appreciate you letting me leave Axel with you," Brianna said, getting back into her car.

She had barely heard half of what Beth was saying to her. Her attention was entirely focused on Ava. Ava was her baby and she looked so small right now, almost curled up in her car seat.

She should have brought Ava to the emergency room earlier, Brianna upbraided herself angrily. Had she waited too long? Had she been too cavalier about her daughter's condition, mistakenly chalking it up to just a cold?

Or had she hesitated bringing Ava in because the health coverage she had wouldn't pay for an ER visit? Since she was self-employed, she had bought the only policy she could afford. The ER fee would go toward her very large deductible and she would have to pay the bill out of her own pocket.

A pocket that was *very* limited, Brianna thought ruefully.

How could she have even thought about money at a time like this? she silently demanded, recriminating tears beginning to fall.

Ava was moaning. It was making her feel even guiltier.

"It's going to be all right, baby. It's going to be all right," Brianna promised. "Mama's going to get you to the hospital and they'll make you all better."

Ava merely moaned again.

She wished that Connor was here. If he was, he could reassure her that everything was going to be all right. She needed to hear his calm, soothing voice, Brianna thought, fighting back the ever-growing feeling of desperation.

But Connor had gone to New Orleans to look up

some more of his extended family. She hadn't been able to reach him the one time she did try.

She hadn't bothered to leave a message. There was no time.

She was on her own, Brianna thought. Just the way she always had been.

"We're going to get through this, honey," she promised her daughter, just as much to bolster Ava as to bolster herself. "And you're going to be better than ever. You'll see."

Brianna prayed she was right.

"Pneumonia?" Brianna repeated the diagnosis numbly. "She has pneumonia?" she asked the weary-looking ER physician. The latter had returned to her with the news once all the results of the tests that had been taken had come in.

The diagnosis still hadn't penetrated. It just didn't make any sense. Ava was just so little. How could she have gotten pneumonia?

"Are you sure?" Brianna asked, her voice all but breaking.

"Very sure," Dr. Valdez replied solemnly. "We're going to have to keep your daughter here at least over-night. She's having trouble breathing," he continued matter-of-factly, "so for now we'll be putting her on oxygen."

"On oxygen?" Brianna echoed. She knew that would frighten Ava. "Is that really necessary?"

"Hopefully, this is just a precautionary measure. But her breathing *is* labored, so before it gets any worse, we need to do this."

Brianna nodded numbly. "Of course. I understand." The words were coming out almost mechanically. She could feel fear all but freezing her vocal cords. "Ava's not—she's not in any danger, is she?" Brianna couldn't get herself to phrase it any differently, afraid to say anything more specific, as if saying the words would make something awful come true.

The doctor's expression softened slightly, as if realizing just how scared she really was.

"There's always a risk in these cases," he told her, "but I think you came here just in time. Is there anyone I can call for you?" he asked. "To come stay with you, or to take you home?" he said gently.

She looked at him blankly for a moment, a mixture of numbness and fear playing tug-of-war with her emotional state. Then, as the doctor's question registered, she shook her head. "No, there's no one," she answered quietly.

Accepting Brianna's answer, the doctor changed the subject. "As soon as we have Ava set up in her room, I'll have a nurse come get you and you can stay with your daughter."

Her room.

She hated saying this, it seemed so crass and petty, especially at a time like this. But she needed to have the doctor aware of her circumstances.

"Doctor, I can't afford to pay for a private room for my daughter."

"Don't worry, the hospital only has single care units for patients. However, the insurance companies process them as if they're semiprivate rooms," he explained.

Brianna wasn't really sure what that meant. Everything seemed to be running together in her head. But she nodded anyway. The important thing was to have her daughter taken care of, and this hospital had the best reputation in the area.

"Thank you, Doctor," she murmured.

She found a chair in the waiting area and sat down.

"Bri, what happened?" Connor cried as he rushed into the room. He looked beside himself with concern.

Exhausted, sleep-deprived—she'd been here for close to twenty-four hours—she looked up at Connor. She didn't even know where to begin, so she just let him go on talking.

"When I didn't find you or the kids at home, I called Beth and she told me that you had taken Ava to the hospital."

Even as he said the words, Connor looked at the sleeping, pale little figure in the hospital bed. They had run out of beds in her size and had put Ava into an adult-size bed for now. She looked even smaller and more helpless in it than she would have appeared in the children's bed.

"What's wrong with her?" he wanted to know, almost afraid of the answer. "Why does she have those tubes running through her?"

He had come back from New Orleans ready to celebrate. The trip to find his newly discovered relatives had gone particularly well. The first thing he'd done once he'd landed was hurry over to see Brianna to share the news with her. When he couldn't find anyone there, he'd grown progressively more worried.

But nothing could have prepared him for this.

Connor felt as if he'd been kicked in the stomach and all the air had been knocked out of him.

"Bri?" he asked when she hadn't answered him yet. "Why is she here?"

"Ava has pneumonia," Brianna began shakily.

"Pneumonia?" Connor echoed. There was an edge in his voice. An edge because fear had seized his gut. He turned to look at Brianna. "Just like that? You didn't see it coming? There was no warning?"

It sounded as if he was accusing her, she thought. She was already taking herself to task over that. She didn't need him making it worse.

"She said she felt achy," Brianna answered. "I thought she had a cold." With each word, she felt guiltier and guiltier that she'd allowed her daughter's condition to get to this stage.

The guilt coupled with anger. She was sleep-deprived and half out of her mind with concern and worry. Brianna felt as if she was backed into a corner.

"There's a difference between a cold and pneumonia," Connor pointed out. All sorts of thoughts began popping up in his head. What if something awful had happened? What if Ava had wound up dying?

The thought suddenly materialized, seizing his heart and haunting him.

Brianna felt as if he was attacking her. Something snapped inside of her. Everything she'd been feeling these last few hours suddenly came pouring out.

"I know that, Einstein," she retorted sarcastically. What right did he have to talk to her this way? Connor hadn't even been here to support her when she needed him the most.

The sight of the little girl, looking so ill, sent a panicky feeling through him. He couldn't take it, couldn't take the thoughts he was struggling to tamp down.

"I'm going out. I need some air," he suddenly said to Brianna.

"Go ahead. Go get your air," she snapped at him. "And while you're at it, just keep on going."

Connor turned to look at her, stunned at the anger he heard in her voice. Stunned at what it sounded like she was telling him. He had to be wrong.

"What are you saying?"

The more she spoke, the angrier she got. She'd been wrong about him. He was bailing at the first sign of a problem. Well, she wasn't going to placidly stand for it. "I'm saying I want you to get out of here. Now!"

"You don't mean that. I just need to get out for a minute," he told her. "Brianna, calm down."

"Calm down?" she shot back, incensed. "Look, you weren't here. I had no one to talk to, no one to turn to and my little girl was sick. I don't have money to run to the doctor every time one of them has a cold. So I gambled and nearly lost my daughter." Angry tears glistened in her eyes.

"Bri—" He reached for her but she pulled away.

"You have no right to criticize me. Now get out of here!"

"Bri—"

"Now!" she insisted.

He looked at Brianna, and then at Ava. All sorts of scenarios filled his head. Scenarios he couldn't deal with. Scenarios that threatened to bring him to his knees.

All he wanted to do right now was get away so he could pull himself together.

"All right," he told Brianna.

And he left.

Chapter Seventeen

When his heart finally stopped racing ninety miles an hour, and the cold, clammy feeling he was experiencing throughout every inch of his body finally receded, Connor was at last able to think more clearly.

He understood now why fear had seized him in such a viselike, death grip.

For several awful minutes, all he could think of was what if Ava had died. He hadn't been here to help Brianna, to give her his support, his money, whatever it took to prevent this from happening, or at least to lessen its impact on Brianna.

If Ava had been taken to see a doctor when all this had started, he felt that it definitely wouldn't have evolved to this degree.

Guilt ate away at him out there in the darkened parking lot.

Seeing a doctor took money, he realized. Picking up and going to see a doctor was something he took for granted. He'd always taken it for granted, he thought ruefully. He hadn't stopped to think what it was like for people in Brianna's circumstances. He'd never had to budget money out of necessity the way he knew Brianna always had.

Damn it, why hadn't he given Brianna money just in case something unforeseen came up while he was gone? He shook his head, annoyed with himself. But he had never had to think that way, so he hadn't.

She wouldn't have taken it anyway, he thought now. Connor felt guilty, helpless and afraid as he got into his car.

At a complete loss what to do with himself, he knew he needed to clear his head as well as calm down before he could approach Brianna again.

Turning on the ignition, he slowly pulled away from the hospital and began to drive home.

The guilt wouldn't leave him alone, threatening to all but consume him.

He should have been here for her. He shouldn't have allowed his obsession to play such a big part in his life, pushing him to meet more and more of his extended family so he could warn them about Charlotte. Who did he think he was, Paul Revere?

The only thing he *had* to do was be here for Brianna and her kids.

The road before him was empty and desolate.

The look on her face haunted him as the sound of her voice ordering him to go away echoed over and over again in his head. He continued driving.

Connor desperately wanted to turn his car around to drive back to the hospital, to apologize to Brianna again for not being there when she needed him. But he knew she needed time. She needed to calm down first. She had been through a crisis—if he felt this awful about almost losing Ava, how much worse was this for Brianna?—and she needed to regain her mental equilibrium before he approached her again.

He wanted her to forgive him, not permanently cut him out of her life. He needed to be patient when patient was the last thing he was.

Blowing out a huge breath, Connor forced himself to continue driving to his parents' house. Things needed to have a chance to settle down.

Everything, he told himself, would be better in the morning.

But it wasn't.

Morning arrived and it was pure agony for him to wait until a decent hour before calling Brianna. As anxious as he was to talk to her, he didn't want to wake her. When he saw her in the hospital room, she had looked really wiped out. She needed her rest.

As for him, Connor had hardly slept all night. He finally gave up trying and got up by five. He was dressed within five minutes, then paced around until eight.

At eight o'clock on the dot, he called Brianna.

His heart sank when he got her voice mail instead of her.

Tempted to hang up, he left a message instead. "Hi, it's me. How is she?" he asked tensely. When he'd left, the prognosis had been positive, but he was taking nothing for granted. "Brianna, I can't tell you how sorry I am that I wasn't here for you. And that I fell apart in the hospital room. You have to understand that—"

A metallic *beep* went off, telling him that his time was up. He was cut off.

Connor dialed again. The same recording came on, telling him to leave a message.

"Bri, I need to talk to you. I have to explain what happened. You need to know that I—"

Another beep. He was cut off again. Apparently only very short messages were to be left.

Frustrated, fearing the worst even as he tried not to jump to conclusions, Connor called the hospital this time, requesting the nurses' station on the pediatric floor.

"Can I speak to the nurse taking care of Ava Childress?" he asked the person who had picked up.

"Just a minute."

Placed on hold, he found himself listening to some song he couldn't identify. It played all the way through, and then started again from the beginning. He was almost all the way through it again when he heard the receiver finally being picked up.

"Hello?"

He talked fast, afraid of being cut off. "I'm calling to find out Ava Childress's condition. She was brought in over a day ago with pneumonia."

"Are you a relative?" the young voice asked him.

Connor hesitated, then was forced to say no, he wasn't.

"Look, I know it's against the rules, but…could you just tell me how she's doing? I'm really worried."

The woman on the other end paused, as if debating what to do. "What did you say your name was?"

"Connor—Connor Fortunado. I'm a good friend of the family." He wasn't used to lying and his heart was pounding. "Please, I really need to know. How's Ava doing?"

The woman looked around to see if anyone was listening. Her expression softened. "She's doing better. I'm sorry, I can't tell you any more than that, though."

Connor closed his eyes. Relief flooded through him like a river swollen with rainwater, making him almost weak.

"Thank you," he told the nurse. "Thank you so much. I can't begin to tell you how grateful I am to hear this news."

The young woman nodded. "If you'll excuse me, I really have to go."

Before Connor had a chance to say another word, the nurse was gone and he found himself listening to a dial tone.

He sighed, drained. At least he knew that Ava was recovering. That she was going to be all right.

Now all he had to do was get her mother to return his calls.

She didn't.

Over the course of the next few days, Connor must have called Brianna at least a dozen times. She never picked up.

Each time he called, he left her a message. She

never returned a single one. He would have gone to see her at the hospital, but he didn't want to cause a scene. Connor was afraid that might upset Ava, and right now, the little girl needed to get well more than he needed to get Brianna to listen to him and forgive him.

To keep from thinking about Brianna, as well as making himself crazy counting the minutes as they dragged by, Connor focused his attention on something else.

Something positive.

It felt as if she'd been gone for an entire month instead of just a few days, Brianna thought when she finally drove up to her home again.

The doctor had pronounced Ava recovered and he had released the little girl from the hospital that morning right after nine.

Parking her car, Brianna got out and came over to the rear passenger side. She was all set to carry Ava from the car into the house, but the little girl pushed her hands away.

"I'm all better, Mama. I can walk," Ava insisted.

Brianna had her doubts, but she didn't want to argue on her daughter's first day back.

"Okay, I'll let you walk into the house, but then you're going straight to bed, young lady. You still need to rest," Brianna told her.

Ava pouted. "But I'm better. The doctor said so," her daughter reminded her.

Apparently things were getting back to normal, Brianna thought. "I know, baby," she said with a smile, "but humor me."

"What's that?" Ava wanted to know, puzzled.

Both of her kids were so precocious, there were times that she forgot she was talking to children, not adults. "It means do as I say, please." They walked up to the front door slowly. Brianna unlocked the door, then paused to look at her daughter. "You gave me quite a scare, baby."

Ava looked up at her, confused. "I'm not scary, Mama."

Brianna laughed and shook her head. "No, not anymore," she agreed. "But you were, baby, you were."

They'd walked in and Ava cocked her head now, listening. "Axel's laughing," she said, recognizing her brother's voice. "Did you tell him I was home?"

"No, not yet," she answered. "We just got in." Brianna paused and listened herself.

There was someone else with her son, she realized. She heard a deep, male voice laughing with Axel.

Beth came out of the kitchen just then. Brianna had told her friend that she was bringing Ava home from the hospital today and asked Beth to come to the house with Axel.

She looked at her friend quizzically now.

Before she could ask, Beth said, "He's been over to my house every day to see Axel while you were in the hospital with Ava. He told me that he didn't want the boy to worry about his sister or to feel like he was being left behind. When I told you were coming home with Ava today, he said he wanted to come with the boy in case you needed help."

Beth smiled at her. "I think you finally have yourself a keeper, Brianna, but that's just me. I left Harry with the kids," she went on, "so I'd better get going. The kids tend to overwhelm him after an hour." She squeezed Brianna's hand, then looked at the little girl. "I'm glad to see you home, Ava."

Ava smiled. "I'm glad to see me home, too," she said to her mother's friend. Turning toward her mother, Ava complained, "They're having fun without me."

"Well, we'll just see about that," Brianna answered. "But you have to promise you're going to lie down very soon."

Ava nodded. "Promise," she answered.

When Brianna walked into the living room with Ava, both Connor and Axel stopped what they were doing.

Axel scrambled up to his feet. "You're back!" he cried. And then, because he didn't want Ava to think he was happy to see her, he said, "I gotta finish playing with Connor."

"Hold on a minute," Connor told the boy. Getting up, he crossed over to Brianna and her daughter. But instead of saying anything to the woman, he first stooped down to Ava's level and pretended to scowl. "What are you doing out of bed, young lady?"

Ava raised her chin. "Doctor said I'm all better."

"Oh, he did, did he? I bet he also said he wanted you to get some rest when you came home," Connor told her. "Am I right?"

Reluctantly, Ava nodded her head and said in a small voice, "Yes."

"I thought so," he said. "Let's get you in bed." He picked Ava up in his arms. And that was when he finally looked at Brianna. "Right, Mama?" he asked her with a smile.

Oh Lord, she'd missed that smile. Missed the sound of his voice, too, Brianna thought. She felt guilty now for the way she'd treated him at the hospital. She'd been so afraid of losing Ava that she had just lashed out at the first target she could find, which in this case turned out to be Connor.

"Right," Brianna answered. She followed Connor to the kids' bedroom.

Ava was asleep before they finished tucking her in.

"I'll stay with her to make sure she doesn't wake up and need something," Axel volunteered, totally surprising his mother.

"You're a real big help, Axel," she told her son, kissing the top of his head.

It was obvious that he was pleased to have his efforts recognized, but Axel pretended to shrug off her words. He dragged over his chair and sat down beside the bottom bunk, a silent sentry watching over his sister.

Connor waited until he and Brianna were both out of the room before he suddenly took her aside and said, "I can't tell you how scared I was when I saw Ava looking so sick that day. I didn't know how to act," he admitted, "and I was afraid to think."

Brianna nodded. She understood that now. "I could see that from your reaction at the hospital," she confessed, "but I thought you felt it was too much for you to handle and that you just wanted to bail."

Connor took her hands in his, grateful beyond words for a second chance.

"I just wanted to catch my breath," he said. "I didn't realize just how much I loved all of you until I saw Ava lying in that hospital bed, looking so tiny and helpless. I'd never been so scared about anything in my life. Scared of losing her. Scared of losing all of you," he emphasized. "That's when I realized that I already thought of us as a family. I'm so sorry I didn't make that clear to you. I had my doubts in the beginning," he admitted, "but not anymore."

This one time in her life, Brianna told herself that she wasn't going to jump to conclusions. "What are you saying exactly?"

His eyes met hers. "What I'm saying is that I love you and I want you to marry me."

"Are you sure?" she asked him. She didn't want to say yes and then have her heart broken again. She couldn't bear it. "I'll understand if you just got swept up in the moment and you want to back out—"

Putting his hand in his pocket, Connor took something out. And as Brianna watched in utter amazement, he got down on one knee, opened the box he'd taken out and offered her what was inside it.

The diamond ring caught the light, winking at her like a flirtatious young girl. Brianna stared at it, her breath caught in her throat.

"Does this look like I want to back out?" Because she was still utterly speechless, Connor went on to tell her, "I'm moving back to Houston for good—and in with you if you'll have me. So what do you say, Bri? Will you marry me?"

"Say yes, Mama! Say yes!"

They turned to see Axel standing in the doorway

with Ava right beside him, eagerly adding her voice to his. Axel had woken her up when he heard Connor talking to his mom.

"I guess it's unanimous," Brianna told Connor with a laugh.

"Good answer," Connor replied. Then he turned toward the children and told them, "I'm going to kiss your mom now, so, Axel, take your sister back to her bed, will you, son?"

Axel giggled in response to being called *son*, and Ava did, too. Taking his sister's hand, he led her back into their bedroom.

"This is as alone as we're going to get," Brianna told Connor.

"Fine with me," he said just before he lowered his lips to hers.

And it really was fine.

For all of them.

* * * * *

Look for Guarding His Fortune *by*
USA TODAY Bestselling Author Stella Bagwell,
the next book in
The Fortunes of Texas: The Lost Fortunes.
On sale April 2019,
wherever Harlequin books and ebooks are sold.

And catch up with the previous books in
The Fortunes of Texas: The Lost Fortunes:

A Deal Made in Texas
by Michelle Major

Her Secret Texas Valentine
by Helen Lacey

Available now!

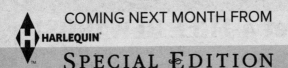
#2683 GUARDING HIS FORTUNE
The Fortunes of Texas: The Lost Fortunes • by Stella Bagwell
Savannah Fortune is off-limits, and bodyguard Chaz Mendoza knows it. The grad student he's been hired to look after is smart, opinionated—and rich. What would she want with a regular guy like Chaz? Her family has made it clear he has no permanent place in her world. But Chaz refuses to settle for anything less...

#2684 THE LAWMAN'S ROMANCE LESSON
Forever, Texas • by Marie Ferrarella
When Shania Stewart tells Deputy Daniel Tallchief that he needs to lighten up with his wild younger sister, the handsome lawman doesn't know whether to ignore her or kiss her. But Shania knows. It's going to take a carefully crafted lesson plan to tutor this cowboy in love.

#2685 TO KEEP HER BABY
The Wyoming Multiples • by Melissa Senate
After Ginger O'Leary learns she's pregnant, it's time for a whole new Ginger. James Gallagher is happy to help, but after years of raising his siblings, becoming attached isn't in the plan. But neither is the way his heart soars every time he and Ginger match wits. What will it take for these two opposites to realize that they're made for each other?

#2686 AN UNEXPECTED PARTNERSHIP
by Teresa Southwick
Leo Wallace had been duped—hard—once before, so he refuses to take Tess's word when she says she's pregnant. Now she wants Leo's help to save her family business, too. Leo agrees to be the partner Tess needs. But it's going to take a paternity test to make him believe this baby is his. He just can't trust his heart again...no matter what it's saying.

#2687 THE NANNY CLAUSE
Furever Yours • by Karen Rose Smith
When Daniel Sutton's daughters rescue an abandoned calico, the hardworking attorney doesn't expect to be sharing his home with a litter of newborns! And animal shelter volunteer Emma Alvarez is transforming the lives of Daniel and his three girls. The first-time nanny is a natural with kids and pets. Will that extend to a single father ready to trust in love again?

#2688 HIS BABY BARGAIN
Texas Legends: The McCabes • by Cathy Gillen Thacker
Ex-soldier turned rancher Matt McCabe wants to help his recently widowed friend and veterinarian, Sara Anderson. She wants him to join her in training service dogs for veterans—oddly, he volunteers to take care of her adorable eight-month-old son, Charley, instead. This "favor" feels more like family every day...though their troubled pasts threaten a happy future.

HSECNM0319

Get 4 FREE REWARDS!

We'll send you 2 FREE Books <u>plus</u> 2 FREE Mystery Gifts.

Harlequin® Special Edition books feature heroines finding the balance between their work life and personal life on the way to finding true love.

FREE Value Over $20

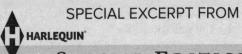
Shania flushed as she raised her eyes toward Daniel. "I
don't usually babble like this."

Daniel found the pink hue that had suddenly risen to
her cheeks rather sweet. The next second, he realized that
he was staring. Daniel forced himself to look away. "I
hadn't noticed."

"Yes, you had," Shania contradicted. "But I think that
it's very nice of you to pretend that you hadn't." When
she heard Daniel laugh softly to himself, she asked him,
"What's so funny?" before she could think to stop herself.

"I'm not accustomed to hearing the word *nice* used to
describe me," he admitted.

Didn't the man have any close friends? Someone to
bolster him up when he was down on himself? "You're
kidding."

The lopsided smile answered her before he did. "Something else I'm not known for."

She pretended that he was a student and she did a quick assessment of the man before her. "You know you're being very hard on yourself."

"Not hard," he contradicted. "Just honest."

She had no intention of letting this slide. If he had been one of her students, she would have done what she could to raise his spirits—or maybe it was his self-esteem that needed help.

"Well, I think you're nice—and you do have a sense of humor."

"If you say so," Daniel replied, not about to dispute the matter. He had a feeling that arguing with Shania would be pointless. "But just so you know, I'm not about to chuck my career and become a stand-up comedian."

She grinned at his words. "See, I told you that you had a sense of humor," she declared happily.

Don't miss
The Lawman's Romance Lesson *by Marie Ferrarella,*
available April 2019 wherever
Harlequin® *Special Edition books and ebooks are sold.*

www.Harlequin.com

Looking for more satisfying love stories
with community and family at their core?

Check out **Harlequin® Special Edition**
and **Love Inspired®** books!

New books available every month!

CONNECT WITH US AT:

Facebook.com/groups/HarlequinConnection

Facebook.com/HarlequinBooks

Twitter.com/HarlequinBooks

Instagram.com/HarlequinBooks

Pinterest.com/HarlequinBooks

ReaderService.com

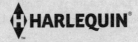

**ROMANCE WHEN
YOU NEED IT**

HFGENRE2018

They'd both just turned back to their work when a familiar loud, croaking sound cut the silence.

The twins shrieked and ran from where they'd been playing into the little cabin's yard and slammed into Anna, their faces frightened.

"What was that?" Anna sounded alarmed, too, kneeling to hold and comfort both girls.

"Nothing to be afraid of," Sean said, trying to hold back laughter. "It's just egrets. Type of water bird." He located the source of the sound, then went over to the trio, knelt beside them, and pointed through the trees and growth.

When the girls saw the stately white birds, they gasped.

"They're so pretty!" Anna said.

"Pretty?" Sean chuckled. "Nobody from around here would get excited about an egret, nor think it's especially pretty." But as he watched another one land beside the first, white wings spread wide as it skidded into the shallow water, he realized that there was beauty there. He just hadn't noticed it before.

That was what kids did for you: made you see the world through their fresh, innocent eyes. A fist of longing clutched inside his chest.

The twins were tugging at Anna's shirt now, trying to get her to take them over toward the birds. "You may go look as long as you can see me," she said, "but take careful steps by the water." She took the bolder twin's face in her hands. "The water's not deep, but I still don't want you to wade in. Do you understand?"

Both little girls nodded vigorously.

They ran off and she watched for a few seconds, then turned back to her work with a barely audible sigh.

"Go take a look with them," he urged her. "It's not every day kids see an egret for the first time."

"You're sure?"

"Go on." He watched her run like a kid over to her girls. And then he couldn't resist walking a few steps closer and watching them, shielded by the trees and brush.

The twins were so excited that they weren't remembering to be quiet. "It caught a *fish*!" the one was crowing, pointing at the bird, which, indeed, held a squirming fish in its mouth.

"That one's neck is like an S!" The quieter twin squatted down, rapt.

Anna eased down onto the sandy beach, obviously unworried about her or the girls getting wet or dirty, laughing and talking to them and sharing their excitement.

The sight of it gave him a melancholy twinge. His own mom had been a nature lover. She'd taken him and his brothers fishing, visited a nature reserve a few times, back in Alabama where they'd lived before coming here.

Oh, if things were different, he'd run with this, see where it led…

Don't miss
Lee Tobin McClain's Low Country Hero,
available March 2019 from HQN Books!

www.Harlequin.com

PHLTMEXP0319

Love Harlequin romance?

DISCOVER.

Be the first to find out about promotions, news and exclusive content!

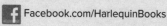

Facebook.com/HarlequinBooks

Twitter.com/HarlequinBooks

Instagram.com/HarlequinBooks

Pinterest.com/HarlequinBooks

ReaderService.com

EXPLORE.

Sign up for the Harlequin e-newsletter and download a free book from any series at **TryHarlequin.com.**

CONNECT.

Join our Harlequin community to share your thoughts and connect with other romance readers!
Facebook.com/groups/HarlequinConnection

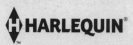

**ROMANCE WHEN
YOU NEED IT**

MEET THE FORTUNES!

Fortune of the Month: Connor Fortunado

Age: 31

Vital Statistics: Tall, sinewy, hazel-eyed charmer. Fearless—except when it comes to falling in love.

Claim to Fame: Everyone thinks he's a corporate researcher, including his family. But he's actually a private investigator. Right now he is trying to track down a Fortune relative who may be up to no good. *(We hope you will be discreet.)*

Romantic Prospects: It's no secret that Connor is a catch. But he's more "flavor of the month" than "till death do us part." A single mom with two preschoolers would definitely not be on the menu.

"Right now my whole life is focused on finding Charlotte Robinson, or at least reaching any of the Fortunes she may be targeting. I really can't afford any distractions, no matter how... distracting. Brianna Childress has been a great help. And man, is she pretty. But... Two kids. A dog. Two cats. A turtle?

"The bottom line is, a man like me needs his freedom. A woman like Brianna needs...more than I can give. I should just stay away from her. So why do I keep coming back?"

* * *

THE FORTUNES OF TEXAS:
The Lost Fortunes—Family secrets revealed!

Dear Reader,

Welcome back to another book about the Fortunes, the family that just keeps on giving. This time we meet Connor Fortunado, who, it turns out, is actually part of the Fortune family. Strange things have been happening to members of the family, so Connor begins to investigate and becomes convinced that Charlotte Robinson is behind everything.

Charlotte was married to the womanizing Gerald Robinson, aka Jerome Fortune. When Gerald left her to marry his "first and only love," Charlotte decided to avenge herself. Now no one knows where she is, but she has left behind a trail of havoc. Determined to find her as well as warn members of his family, Connor tracks down Brianna Childress, a single mother of two very precocious children, and discovers that she had done some work for Charlotte. He seeks her out, determined to convince her to help him find his target. What he finds instead is the one thing he wasn't looking for: a woman to complete him, and just maybe a family, too.

I hope you enjoy reading this as much as I enjoyed writing it. I confess I have a great weakness for short people (otherwise known as little kids). As always, I thank you for taking the time to read one of my books, and from the bottom of my heart, I wish you someone to love who loves you back.

All the best,

Marie

Texan Seeks Fortune

―

Marie Ferrarella

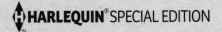
HARLEQUIN® SPECIAL EDITION

Special thanks and acknowledgment are given
to Marie Ferrarella for her contribution to
the Fortunes of Texas: The Lost Fortunes series.

Recycling programs
for this product may
not exist in your area.

ISBN-13: 978-1-335-57370-4

Texan Seeks Fortune

Printed in U.S.A.